Dying For Dirt (All Soaped Up)

(A Tucson Valley Retirement Community Cozy Mystery)

By: Marcy Blesy

This book is a work of fiction. Names, characters, places, and events are a result of the imagination of the author or are used fictitiously. Any resemblance to actual persons, living or dead, businesses, events, or locations is a coincidence.

No part of the text may be reproduced without the written permission of the author, except for brief passages in reviews.

Copyright © 2024 by Marcy Blesy, LLC. All rights reserved.

Cover design by Cormar Covers

# Chapter 1

"Yes, Mom. My flight was fine. Nope, I didn't have to take a middle seat. Nope. I had an aisle seat. I didn't mind. Zak is staying with Wes for a few days before going back to Chicago. He's taking summer classes. No girlfriend that I know of. I've got to go, Mom. Yes, I'll squeeze Barley for you. Tell Dad hello. Love you, too." I set down my phone and collapse into my new bright yellow cushioned chair, swinging my legs onto the ottoman. Barley jumps onto my lap once I am settled. I stare out my sliding back door onto the Santa Rita Mountains. The bright hot, hot, hot sun is beating down on my backyard this time of day, the only part of shade being the tiny corner between the back of my condo unit's garage wall and where it meets my living room at a perpendicular angle. Barley claims the cushioned chair in that corner as hers anytime she's forced to spend time outdoors, which isn't much this August. If I were being honest, adjusting to the summer months in the Southwest has kicked my butt. It literally takes my breath away to walk outside in the afternoon on my way home from work. I don't know how Keaton can work outside all day as a landscaper. Dad had given him five new icy scarves with stern instructions to dump them in cold water and to reapply throughout the day. Keaton said he'd never been more touched by a gift.

I pick up a book that I'd been reading on the airplane back from Illinois, but I can't get into the spicy romance. My mind wanders back to my busy week. The house I'd shared with Wes for nearly twenty years had sold quickly once I'd settled on a financial arrangement that he accepted. I spent the week going through the things that remained in the house, most of Wes's things having been taken when he'd moved out but downsizing from a 3000 square foot home to a two-bedroom condo isn't an easy task emotionally or physically. Dad watched Flynn and Hudson when Simon was at work, and Mom, Shelly, and I worked methodically to put items into categories: donation, trash, Tucson Valley, storage in Springfield. Ivy was mesmerized by all of the commotion as she sat in her activity saucer watching us work. Simon and Shelly hit the jackpot in baby temperaments when they had her.

Of course, the Tucson Valley pile had to be able to fit into my car and the small trailer I'd rented to pull behind me in my new car. I'd sold my Illinois car to Zak's old high school basketball buddy for $6500. I'd followed Zak to

4

Chicago to deliver the car to his friend who'd also left central Illinois for the bright lights of the big city. That gave us a chance to talk all the way back to Springfield since he'd agreed to help us move some of the bigger pieces of furniture. He'd even taken a few days off from his part-time job interning in the sales department at the United Center in between classes. It was the second semester he'd interned there. Forced to be in a car with me for three hours, he couldn't scroll on his phone without being rude or run out for an *errand*. And it had been amazing. He'd talked about his job, about his life goals to run a professional sports organization *(Why not aim big?)*, about how he was nervous about his senior project coming up in the fall, about his crush on a bright young lady who worked at the Shedd Aquarium and fed the penguins every day. He'd asked me questions, too, about my job and Tucson Valley and about Keaton. I'd introduced them via FaceTime in early summer after I learned that Zak wouldn't have time to fly down to Arizona over the summer. They'd truly vibed, as Zak had told me afterwards. I'd taken that to mean something positive then, and as we passed the corn growing tall in the fields along I-57, Zak told me that he'd never seen me smile so much and that he was genuinely

5

happy for me. I didn't ask him if that's how his dad acted with Cara, too, but I imagine the answer would have been *yes*.

*Answer your doorbell.*

Huh? I read my text message. Just then the doorbell rings. I peek through the blinds and see Keats standing there with a huge bouquet of flowers in his hands. I open the door, and he thrusts the flowers into my hands.

"Welcome home, Rosi."

"Thanks, Keats. The flowers are beautiful, but what's the occasion?"

"I'm just trying to ensure you know how much you were missed so you don't go trying to leave more often on me or something like that."

"I don't think you need to worry." I lean over the flowers and plant a big kiss on his lips. "No more trips in my future. And I've missed you, too."

"Good because I have big plans for us the rest of the summer!"

Keaton only makes it a few steps into the condo before Barley is all over him. She jumps up and down over and over, nipping at the bottom of his shirt until Keats bends over and scoops her up, all forty pounds. "Hey, girl.

Did you miss me?" Barley slobbers Keaton's face with a wet kiss.

"Well, you got your answer," I say as I put the roses, sunflowers, and lilies bouquet into a glass vase on my kitchen island.

"Did she behave for Mario and Celia?" he asks as he plops onto my new chair. Barley jumps on his stomach, spins around three times, and settles on his chest as Keaton leans back in the chair, her bottom smashing against his chin.

"Celia was an absolute doll when I picked Barley up. She kept gushing on and on about how grateful she was that I'd let them keep Barley for the week."

"And how did he do with their grandson?"

"Apparently, Barley and Vick got on famously."

"That's awesome."

"I agree. With his disability, life can be challenging, but they said that they'd never seen Vick smile so much as when Barley was in the room.

"Do you think Vick's parents will get him a dog now?"

"Mario thinks a dog would be the best medicine for the little guy. He was even making the 'B' sound the last time he visited their house every time he pointed at Barley. Speech is a huge issue with his disability according to Celia."

"Barley the service dog. Who knew?" asks Keaton as Barley scoots backwards on Keaton's chest until her bottom is now firmly planted in his right cheek, Barley's *cheek* to Keaton's cheek.

"Let's not go *that* far," I laugh.

My phone dings. I pick it up off the coffee table where I'd left it after my call with Mom.

*Exciting news. Pack your bags again! The stipend for the Senior Living Retirement Community Conference in Phoenix just got approved. We leave in three days. Woo! Hoo!*

"Who was that?" Keats asks as the color surely drains out of my face.

I look up at Keaton and shrug my shoulders. "Well, uh, I guess I was a bit premature with my promise of no more trips. I'm going to an old folk's convention. Yay?" I say sarcastically.

Keaton sighs and drops his head onto Barley's butt. "At le…do… laund…bef…you…," he says against Barley's fur as he points his finger blindly in my direction.

"What? I can't understand you."

He lifts his head as Barley pivots 180 degrees so that her butt is facing me now. "I said, *at least do laundry before you pack again because you have a giant ketchup stain on your shirt. Unless you've discovered another dead body and that's blood.*"

"Not funny!" I look down at my shirt and lift it to my nose, sniffing. "Yep, it's ketchup from the hotdog I ate at the last rest area."

Keaton gently pushes Barley off his lap. "Hey, do that again," he says.

"Huh?"

"That thing, with your shirt. Lift it up again."

I toss a yellow and white daisy-printed pillow at his head, and he scoops me up for a passionate kiss. "I think you need another send-off party." He winks at me.

"I guess I need to plan more trips." He carries me into the bedroom where we shut the door, leaving Barley pouting on the other side.

## Chapter 2

Tracy is running around the senior center like a chicken with its head cut off. I've seen her pass by my office at least five times in the last hour. The Tucson Valley Retirement Community Senior Center connects several facilities including the performing arts center—where most of my work is focused—the aquatic center, the sports center, and the café. We are bursting at the seams as none of these divisions is particularly large, and Tucson Valley's population is nearly full. One of the things we will be studying at the Senior Living Retirement Community Conference in Phoenix is how to make the most of the space we have. Of the two of us, I am the organizer. Tracy is a visionary, but she stinks at lining up the details to make that vision come to fruition. That's my job.

"Hey!" I yell at Tracy as she passes by a sixth time.

"Oh, hi, Rosi. What's up?" she asks, sticking her head in my office. Her curls take up nearly a third of the doorway as Tracy's grown out her dirty blonde hair so much so that her curls have taken on a life of their own, providing a sort of protective helmet for her head. It's a wild look. There's no nice way to put it.

"I was hoping we could go over the itinerary before we leave, seeing as we may have different paths once we land in Phoenix."

"Sure. That's a good idea actually. Let me see," she rifles through a stack of file folders, pulling out a red one that she slaps on my desk. She drops the others onto an empty chair and sinks into a black leather chair across from my desk, a gift from my parents before they left. She opens the red folder and pulls out a set of papers. She puts on a pair of yellow reading glasses that had been buried somewhere in her hair and reads from the top sheet. *"The tenth annual Senior Living Retirement Community Conference in Phoenix brings together the best and brightest in the senior living industry to share information, highlight new advances, and teach retirement communities how to offer quality of life options that will be the envy of all retirees across the nation."*

"That's quite an agenda," I say, raising an eyebrow.

"I haven't been to this conference since my first year on the job seven years ago. We have a great product here in Tucson Valley, but there's always room for improvement, right? We could benefit from finding ways to improve upon the opportunities we offer." She takes a deep breath, probably the first time she's sat still for more than five minutes today.

"I think the concept is fascinating. Have you gotten the final list of people who are attending from Tucson Valley?"

"Oh, yes. Sorry I didn't forward that to you." She thumbs through the papers until she pulls out one with a list of names and hands it to me.

"Huh," is all I can say when the names are reflecting back at me.

"Now, Rosi, I know it's not ideal." Tracy taps her foot back and forth against the leg of the chair. "But I didn't have much control. The HOA board, the governing board of all of the Tucson Valley Retirement Community, got much of the choice. You understand that, right?" She looks at me pleading with her eyes for me to play nice and accept my fate.

"Sure."

"Rosi, come on. Please be happy. Mario, you, and I are going to have so much fun together! Mario can't stop smiling with his new title: *Director of Maintenance and Facilities.*

I haven't seen that man so happy since the Toxicity Nemesis followed him back on TikTok."

"Mario is on TikTok?" I don't even ask about who the Toxicity Nemesis is. "Okay, I'll do my best to be excited about this list." I stare at the names in front of me. Brenda Riker and Jan Jinkins, two of Mom's *friends*. Neither woman has ever said a kind word to me, and each could battle for the title of loudest gossiper in Tucson Valley, but I understand why the names are there. Jan represents the coalition of snowbirds for Tucson Valley. She's flying into Tucson Valley from Northwest Illinois to be at the convention. And Brenda is running for mayor of Tucson Valley against Leo Lestman, the acting mayor since Troy Kettleman is now in jail for murder. Leo's name is also on the list. That should be fun. "Why is Safia Devereaux coming?" I ask about my eccentric realtor with the big personality.

"Retirement communities aren't just a way of life for retirees. They are a big business, and Safia is a rockstar when it comes to selling homes in and out of the retirement community. I'd love to expand our property if ever possible, and she'd be a huge help if that opportunity ever comes up."

"Okay, that makes sense. Are there chances to expand?"

Tracy shakes her head sadly. "Not at the moment. We are pretty landlocked by other properties, but I'm working on something top secret. Stay tuned."

"I'll stay tuned, Tracy. When should I be ready to leave?"

She points to the folder. "You'll find the itinerary with times all spelled out. You will be quite impressed. I worked hard on that piece. Your organizational abilities are rubbing off on me."

"Thanks, Tracy, I'll look it over." She gets up to leave. "And I'm really excited about this trip," I say as she gets to the door.

"We are going to have a blast, Rosi! A blast! Now I'm off to the Mabel Brown Sports Complex. Apparently, the toaster ovens in the café keep setting off the fire alarms! See ya!"

Once she is gone, I crumple my upper body onto my desk, feeling defeated. There is not a single bit of this conference I am *really excited* about. Not one single bit. But I need to put on my game face, not let Brenda and Jan get to me, not let Safia annoy me, not let Tracy distract me.

Maybe Leo and Mario will be my saving graces. At least they haven't done anything to sour my thoughts yet. Maybe I need to fix *me* and my sour thoughts' maker. It's working overtime right now.

# Chapter 3

"Are you sure you are up for this?" asks Keaton as he tightens his hiking boots.

It's 5:00 in the morning, and we are about to hike the Ventana Canyon Trail in Tucson. I am leaving tonight for Phoenix, and Keats planned a nice date for us, but because of the blasted inferno that is Arizona in the summer, we have to do all outdoor activities at the crack of dawn. I don't mind physical activities, but if I were being completely truthful with Keaton, I'd have told him I'd rather be getting a massage at the spa we passed coming up the road to the trailhead parking lot. But I'm not truthful. "Sure. Should be fun."

"Do you have your extra water bottle? That sun is going to be intense as it rises in the sky."

I hold up my 36 ounce water bottle and add it to my backpack that holds another smaller water bottle. I'm wearing a tank top and shorts, but already my armpits are getting sticky. I am wondering if my deodorant will hold up when I realize Keaton has taken off. We'd left Barley at home. Keaton had scared me with talk of hopping rocks and passing by cacti. And if Barley caught sight of a wild javelina on the trail she'd be lost to the overgrowth chasing after them.

The first part of the trail snakes along a residential apartment building with a wide, rock-covered path, so I am starting to think that Keaton oversold the difficulty of the trail. But within twenty minutes, the trail narrows and we are climbing over and around rocks on narrow paths with cacti and pricker bushes (my name as Keaton knows the proper names of all of the vegetation). The quick downpour we'd had for a couple of hours last night created tiny pools of water that provide extra fun obstacles when the slippery rocks must be crossed to avoid walking through the water.

"You're doing great, Rosi. Only a few more turns and we will begin to see the vistas in the valley below Tucson."

I want to say, *can't we just have stayed in Tucson VALLEY to see the valley?* but I don't say anything. When a couple in their sixties with walking sticks passes us up, I dig deep inside and give myself a pep talk like Dad used to do when he coached my basketball team in fifth grade. "Look inside, Rosi. Find the drive. You just have to release it."

"Can we stop for a quick drink break? I want to be fueled up for the next play."

"The next play?" Keaton asks, looking at me quizzically.

"Oops, sorry. I mean, the next part of the trail." We sit atop a rock next to the trail and take out our water bottles. From the rock, we can see into the valley below as the sun is starting to rise. Soon, the sun will cover us on the trail, but for now we are in the shadows. "This is pretty fantastic."

Keaton slips his arm around my back and pulls me close to his side. "I've wanted you to see this part of Arizona since that first week I met you."

"What do you mean?" I ask, giving him a side-eye look.

"Something this beautiful should be shared with someone *this* beautiful," Keats says as he kisses me on the cheek.

I feel like the sun's rays are crossing over us now, but it's just the heat rising up my face as Keaton's words settle on my heart. "I'm glad you dragged me out here." This time I mean it.

After sufficiently rehydrating, I readjust my backpack onto my back and allow Keaton to pull me up from the rock. We continue on for another fifteen minutes up the trail, careful to place out feet on sturdy rocks so as not to twist an ankle. The last thing I want to do is spend my time at the convention with a twisted ankle and crutches.

Keaton whistles Taylor Swift songs as we hike. He begins to sing the lyrics to "Cruel Summer" as we approach our next obstacle. A small stream with shallow running water crosses our path, but there are large, uneven rocks in the middle of the stream that form a sort of bridge. Feeling empowered by the sun that is churning up the heat, I take an aggressive hop on the first rock. No problem. I hop to the second rock. I turn around to see Keaton smiling at me, amused by my confidence. Third rock. I'm a natural. It's when I hop onto the final rock that I misjudge the solidness of the rock that is not at all firmly placed in the bed of the creek. It wobbles left as I wobble right to keep my phone that is in the side pocket of my yoga shorts from getting wet, and it's the mismanagement of weight distribution that sends me falling forward into the stream and soaking the right side of my body.

"Rosi!"

I shake my head side to side. I don't need help. I am standing in water no deeper than my shins.

"Are you okay?"

"Bruised but okay. I'm sorry." I look at Keaton who has walked adeptly across the rocks and is holding out his hand from the other side of the water to assist me out of my mess. "Thanks," I say as I take his hand. "That wasn't my plan."

Keaton laughs, "Well, the positive is that you saved your phone and refreshed yourself as it's starting to get hot out. Should we head back?"

"How much longer until we are at the summit?" I put my hand over the top of my eyes to shade them as I squint up the trail. The older couple who passed us earlier are descending.

"Not too much longer!" says the woman. Her makeup hasn't smeared in the least. I wonder if she's even cracked a sweat.

"Did you take a spill?" asks the man as he passes us easily on the rocks in the stream.

"Just a misstep," says Keaton protectively.

"Maybe it's time for a walking stick," the woman says as she raises hers in the air.

I want to push her over, but I don't. "I'll take it under advisement."

Keaton reaches out his hand. "Come on. We're almost there."

I take his hand and follow him up the trail, ignoring the aches in my body that tell me that the old lady was right, and my follies of youthful days are in the past. After ten more minutes, Keaton stops walking. He gestures toward the valley below, full of saguaro cacti, barrel cacti, and mesquite trees. There are no signs of civilization except for a scattering of large houses tucked into the peaks overlooking the valley below. I lean against a rock behind me, exhausted by the trek but in awe of what's before me. But when I reach for my backpack, I'm met with a sharp pain. "Ouch! Son-of-a..." I sink to the ground. I don't mean to cry, but I do. The tears slide down my cheeks, refreshing my warm face.

Keaton sits on the ground next to me. He takes my hand gently into his and removes the cacti spines from my palm as he did once before when I'd tripped over rocks in a park he was landscaping and landed in a cactus bush. He doesn't say anything for a few minutes as I silently cry. When I'm done, he grabs my good hand and squeezes it.

"Rosi, I'm sorry."

"Why...why are you sorry?" I ask softly.

"Because you didn't want to hike, and you did it for me."

"I did want to...I did," I say softly before admitting the truth. "I didn't want to hike. It's true, but once we got going and I saw how beautiful it was, I was really glad to be here. I mean it, Keats. I'm not crying because I'm upset that we are hiking. I am upset because I'm an old lady walking disaster." I whip my head back, but I forget it's a rock I'm leaning against and not my comfy new chair. "Ohhh!"

Keaton grabs me in a bear hug and pulls me toward his chest as he rubs my head gently. "Let's get you off this mountain. You have a big trip today."

"Ugh! Don't remind me. Can't we just stay here and stare at nature. If I don't move any part of my body, I surely can't be hurt."

"Well, that's not necessarily true."

"What do you mean?"

"The snakes will wake up eventually." He shrugs his shoulders.

"Time to go!" I jump up, grab my backpack, and start walking down the trail in one fluid motion.

Keaton soothes my hurt pride by taking me to Dairy Queen. I order a large Cookie Dough Blizzard while he orders a Peanut Buster Parfait. "I *do* want to hike with you again," I say, trying to convince myself as I speak the words aloud.

"Rosi, we don't have to like the same things all of the time." He steals a bite of my Blizzard.

"I know. We've both been so busy with work, though, that it was nice to get out and do something. Maybe we'll try hiking with a little less elevation next time."

Keaton laughs, "I can agree to that. But you won't get the same view."

"True, but I like the view I have right here." I slap my spoon over his nose and watch the ice cream melt off the end. "We have to go! I need to finish packing!"

## Chapter 4

"Are you sure you don't want me to keep Barley for you?"

"I'm sure. She still hasn't forgiven me for loaning her to Mario when I went to Illinois for a week. And even though Mario's grandchild bonded fantastically with her, Barley doesn't want the extra stimulation of a child. After the initial excitement, she crashes. I've checked with the hotel as well as my van mates, and dogs are allowed—welcome, even. The hotel has a fenced in area for dogs to do their business. All of the meetings are in the same building, so I'll be able to visit her in between functions. Plus, there's a mini balcony. She will love it. But I do appreciate your offer. And I am *positive* that Ruthie is happy with this decision. Has she stopped peeing outside of the litter box after the last time Barley visited?"

"Ruthie stopped misbehaving the second Barley left," Keaton laughs. "But that doesn't mean that I want you and Barley to stop visiting." He wraps his arms around me and hugs me tightly. "I'm going to miss you, Rosisophia Doroche Laruee."

"And I will miss you, Alex P. Keaton, but I will only be gone a few days this time. And when I get back, let's do that skygazing camping trip you've been talking about."

He raises a skeptical eyebrow. "Are you sure? It involves a tiny bit of hiking. And sleeping outside."

"Well, yeah, but sleeping in a *tent,* right? Not, like, on the hard ground surrounded by snakes and scorpions?"

"Eventually, but you can't stargaze from *inside* the tent," he grins. And he kisses me on the lips so long that I forget what we are talking about.

The Tucson Valley Retirement Community HOA board, who is paying for our conference, has provided two vans for our travel to and from Phoenix. Tracy, Mario, Barley, and I are traveling in one van. Thankfully, the presence of Barley swayed Safia to take the van with Brenda, Jan, and Leo. I imagine Leo preferred our van, too, but he was running late, and we left ten minutes earlier than the scheduled departure time to gas up. I am driving so that Tracy can go over our agenda again. Barley is quite content to lay across Mario's lap in the middle row.

"I have a file folder for each of you," says Tracy.

"Naturally," I say.

"And you will find a list of the sessions you each chose inside the folder along with information about time and location. Tonight, there is a welcome reception followed by the opening speaker."

"Is there food at the reception?" Mario asks.

"Uh, let me check." Tracy flips through the papers inside her own folder. "Aw, yes. There are light hors d'oeuvres."

"So, uh, treats?" asks Mario.

Barley starts barking.

"Uh-oh, now you've done it," I say, smiling. "There's a dog bone in the side of my black bag if you want to give her a treat now."

"I guess, Mario," says Tracy. "Little finger food appetizers, I imagine, so you can eat and mingle."

"Mingle? Is that something that a Director of Maintenance and Facilities is required to do?"

I can hear the trepidation in his voice. "You can hang out with me, Mario."

"Thanks, Rosi."

"So, what's your greatest desire for this conference, Tracy?"

She nods her head up and down as if deep in thought, her curls remaining firmly in place, though held less wild by two large butterfly barrettes on each side of her head. "I am quite excited for the session about how to do more with less."

"That should be rollicking fun," says Mario sarcastically.

"Ha! Fun wasn't my word, but with our space for expansion limited, we have to get more creative about how to offer more programs with less money *and* less space."

"I think it sounds like a very timely session," I say as we pass a couple in a very slow-moving vintage Rolls Royce out for a Sunday drive on a fast-paced interstate.

"Of course, the opening session with Dr. Rafferty Smith should be smashingly entertaining."

"Who's that?" Marios asks. I glance in my rearview mirror and observe Barley sprawled on her back receiving a belly rub.

"He's an expert in geriatric care—quite popular with the demographic of a retirement community. Let's just say he makes an entrance. And this year he's talking about his new book *Actively Aging: Designing Your Retirement Community for the 100-Year-Old Resident.*"

27

"I don't know too many 100-year-old residents in Tucson Valley," I say.

"Not now, no, but with advances in medicine, people are living longer, and retirement communities need to be prepared to meet the needs of the older population, not just the spry sixty and seventy year olds."

"What sessions are you attending, Rosi?" asks Mario.

"Well, I can't look at my file folder as I'm driving, but I know that I picked out a social media marketing meeting along with a meet-and-greet of potential entertainers for the performing arts center. Oh, and I'm going to a holiday-themed session to get new ideas for marketing and programming."

"This is going to be so much fun!" squeals Tracy.

Mario and I exchange looks of amusement through the rearview mirror. "What about you, Mario?"

I hear shuffling of papers before he speaks. "*Regulations and Rules to Streamline Sanitation* and then, uh, *Safety and Security*. I think your sessions sound more fun."

"I agree!" Tracy and I share a laugh as a van goes barreling past us on the left side. "Crap!" I swerve our van to the shoulder of the road to avoid a collision only to

28

watch the van cross in front of us and come to a screeching halt in the shoulder a half a mile down the road.

"Rosi! That's Jan's van!" yells Tracy.

I check my mirrors. "Hold on to Barley!" I decelerate after making sure that there are no cars directly behind me, pass by Jan's van on the side of the interstate, and pull over fifty yards in front of her van.

"What should we do?" asks Tracy.

"We need to see if they're okay." It seems obvious to me.

"You take Barley. I'll go check." Mario is already undoing his seatbelt. "It's not safe to have extra people walking close to a major interstate."

I nod my head and beckon Barley to jump on my lap. "That was crazy."

Tracy's eyes are big as saucers. She's looking out of the back of our van as if entranced. "Uh oh."

"What's the matter?" I turn around to see Mario dragging luggage through the rocks aside the interstate. Jan, Brenda, Safia, and Leo follow behind, all of them also carrying their luggage. A sinking sense of dread drops from my head to my toes.

"This is going to be...interesting?" Tracy doesn't like Jan or Brenda any more than I do.

I hold tight to Barley's leash, but that doesn't stop her from barking incessantly when the sliding door to the van opens and Jan, Brenda, and Safia get in leaving Mario and Leo to stuff the extra luggage into the back of the van. They are also forced to squeeze into the back row as Brenda, Jan, and Safia take over the middle seat. I pass Barley to Tracy. She immediately slobbers a wet kiss across Tracy's nose.

"What happened?" Tracy asks, turning to our new passengers.

"Well, it's that van you gave us! It went crazy, flying across the road. Didn't you see us? Why, my tire just snapped off!" She puts her hand on her heart as she breathes heavily.

"We saw our lives flash before our eyes, Rosi!" adds Safia, her tortoise-shell glasses sitting atop her head and her floor-length black skirt gathering dog hair from Barley's blanket that is still on the seat.

"I imagine you knew about this—*malfunction,*" Brenda says, staring me square in my eyes.

"Why would *I* know anything about your van's *tire malfunction* issue?"

Barley barks in my defense at a hawk she sees outside the window.

"For all I know, it was driver error that nearly got yourselves killed!"

I hear the sudden sucking in of air from Jan the minute I've said aloud what I should have kept to my own thoughts.

"Ladies, let's settle down. We've all experienced some trauma today," says Leo from the back seat where he sits with his knees bunched up behind the middle row. At well over 6 feet and with a healthy girth around the middle, he is not made for a back row seat.

"Tracy, I'll call the HOA board and let them know what happened and arrange a tow back to Tucson Valley."

"Thanks, Leo," she yells from the front seat.

Leo Lestman is the acting mayor of Tucson Valley, ever since Troy Kettleman got himself into hot water, but there's a special election coming up in a few weeks, August 7th, to be exact, and he and Brenda are in a heated duel for the title of *mayor*, not *acting* anything.

"And *I* will call the board and let them know about the tire sabotage we experienced on the interstate that nearly took our lives!" yells Brenda as she turns around to face Leo, his mustache moving in frustration above his lip.

Barley, not used to incessant yelling, jumps off Tracy's lap and into Brenda's where she bares her teeth and growls. I have never seen her growl at anything other than other four-legged creatures. "Barley!"

"Get this mangy beast off of me!" she shrieks, pushing Barley to the floor of the van.

"Don't hurt my dog!"

"Ladies!" Mario's voice echoes off the walls of the van. "We have things to do. We are all safe. Can we *please* continue on to Phoenix?"

"If Rosi would just start the dang van, we'd be on our way," says Jan.

Safia, not known for quiet, hasn't said a word. Tracy notices, too. "Safia, are you okay?" she asks softly as Safia stares down at her lap, a wild-eyed look of horror on her face.

She nods her head at Tracy but looks at me. "What is it, Safia?" I ask.

32

She turns around to look at the men in the back row. "Can you please cover your ears for a moment?" she asks them.

They wrinkle their foreheads in simultaneous confusion but do as she requests. Then she looks at me again. "I tinkled myself," she whispers.

"Oh, well, I guess that scary things like what you've been through can…"

"Oh, for freaks' sake, can this day get any worse? Now, I'm sitting next to a human toilet?" says Brenda as she looks at Safia in disgust while Jan pats her leg in support.

Safia bursts into tears. "It happens sometimes. I…I didn't mean…" She pulls up the bottom of her long skirt and dabs her eyes with it.

"We can stop at the next rest area, and you can change. Does that sound okay, Safia?"

She nods her head slightly while turning her back on Jan and Brenda who alternate between rolling their eyes and sighing loudly. I have never been so frustrated with two human beings' lack of empathy than I am right now, but Tracy's soft touch on my arm, and Barley's lick on my hand

33

lower my temperature. I push the start button, and we are off on our trip to Phoenix with a quick pit stop first.

An hour later when we pull up to the Phoenix Emporium Hotel and Convention Center, I am in need of a stiff drink, and Safia keeps muttering about needing time to meditate. The arguments hadn't stopped just because we'd started to move again. The men complained of being hot in the back of the van, and Jan and Brenda complained of being treated to Arctic Circle temperatures. Safia was so anxious that she started biting her fingernails—*audibly*—and Jan gagged into the side of her arm threatening to throw up if she didn't stop immediately. We caught up to the old couple in the Rolls Royce again, and I punished myself for my judgement of them and wished with all my might that I was riding in their tiny backseat instead of driving to a senior citizen conference with a bunch of mismatched quirky people.

I take Barley to the fenced-in dog area next to the hotel while Tracy checks in. Mario and Leo unload the luggage. Safia carries her own luggage, resting her bags on top of her rolling suitcase, but Jan and Brenda have commissioned the help of a handsome bellboy to load their items onto a luggage rack. I bet they won't even tip.

When we've all reconvened in the lobby, Tracy passes out our keys. "Jan, Brenda, and Safia, you are in room 223, Rosi's in room 221 with Barley," she pauses to pat the top of Barley's head. "Mario and Leo are in room 225, and I am in room 227."

"Why on Earth are some of us sharing rooms and you and Rosi get your own rooms?" asks Jan, her head shaking from side to side so quickly that it might fall off her body.

"The HOA board made the room assignments, Jan. Take it up with them." Tracy walks away from the chaos, dragging her suitcase behind her. She and Barley and I take the elevator without them to the second floor.

## Chapter 5

"Meet me in thirty minutes, Rosi?" Tracy asks, her butterfly barrette falling out of her hair as if it's about to take flight.

"Yeah, sure. What's the attire for the reception and opening speaker?"

"It's in the folder. You'll see." She smiles, but I see the tired eyes that are second guessing the choice of attendees from our coalition.

"It's going to be okay, Tracy. We're going to have a great time and learn a lot to help our residents in Tucson Valley."

"Thanks, Rosi. Thank goodness for you and Mario."

Barley immediately jumps into the middle of my queen bed, rotates exactly three times, and drops into the mess of comforter she's disrupted. Within a minute, she is snoring. Everyone's stress level (including Barley's) accelerated faster than Jan's foot on the gas when her tire fell off and her car flew across the lanes of traffic on the interstate.

I lay down on the bed next to Barley and pull out my folder to read about my evening.

*The Senior Living Retirement Community Conference invites you to attend our opening night reception in the Lystila Banquet Hall from 5:30-6:45 where light hors d'oeuvres and drinks will be served. Attendees will be allotted two cocktail coupons. At exactly 7:00, the opening ceremonies will begin with a recap of the Southwest Senior Living Board's activities from the past year followed by our guest speaker. Dr. Rafferty Smith is the author of the new bestseller, Actively Aging: Designing Your Retirement Community for the 100-Year-Old Resident. He earned a PHD from the University of Michigan in geriatric care and founded the smashingly popular singing group, the Screamin' Seniors, a cover band with all members over the age of 75.*

I skim the rest of the man's accolades to find the dress code. *Business Casual.* After a quick call with Keaton, I drag myself to the bathroom where I run a comb through my long hair. I click on the curling iron to curl the ends under and touch up my makeup while the iron is heating. The bathroom is surprisingly large, and I look longingly at the bathtub wishing I could stay there with a good book,

37

bubble bath, and a glass of wine instead of networking. But I know my mission, and I won't let Tracy down.

I choose a new pair of navy pants, a cream tank top, and a short navy blazer because conference rooms are notorious for being cold even when held in late July in Phoenix. I finish my hair, add a pair of silver hoops, and apply a fresh coat of lip gloss. I assess myself in the mirror. When I am satisfied, I fill Barley's water and food bowls. She still snores, not even lifting her head as I find my nametag in my folder: *Rosi Laruee, Tucson Valley Retirement Community,* and put it over my neck. I grab my key and meet Tracy for our elevator ride to the reception.

Tracy looks nicer than I have ever seen her before. She's wearing an emerald green sleeveless dress that falls at her knees with a white sweater shrug, and her wild curls are smoothed with gel and held together in a low ponytail at the nape of her neck. I think she might even be wearing perfume, but I don't ask her. "Rosi, I have a business meeting. I'm going to have to miss the reception, but I'll meet you at the opening ceremony. Can you save me a seat?"

"Okay. I'll be in the back. I don't need anyone from the stage calling on me," I laugh nervously because I sure didn't see anything in my file folder about a business meeting to be held during the reception. Tracy's husband is a long-haul truck driver, and he's gone a lot. I sure hope Tracy doesn't have any naughty plans for this conference. If she does, the less I know, the better.

I watch Tracy walk toward the lobby of the hotel while I look for the Lystila Banquet Hall. Mario and Leo are each drinking a bottle of beer and eating finger foods that look like stuffed mushrooms and ham, pickle, and cream cheese wraps from the bits that remain on their paper plates that sit on the high-top tables.

"Hi, Rosi," says Leo who is grabbing a mini-cheeseburger slider off the tray of a passing waiter. Leo is wearing a short-sleeve, button-down white shirt with a purple tie that matches the pocket square in his shirt. From my quick observations around the room, he isn't the only man wearing a tie.

"Hello, Leo. How's the food?"

"Great!" He wipes a crumb from his mustache, and it lands on the sleeve of my blazer. I pick up a napkin and knock it to the ground. "Food is delish. Room is the bomb, and I don't have to talk to Brenda for the next two days!"

Mario, who is wearing a tasteful black polo and khaki pants, laughs. I join them because, I, too, hope to avoid Brenda for the next forty-eight hours. Speaking of the devils, we all turn our heads as we watch them walk by our table without so much as a glance. Brenda wears a slinky light pink dress and two inch black heels. She clearly has more hair than she did an hour ago. I wonder if it's clip-ins or a full-on wig. What I would give to tug on that hair to answer my question. Jan is wearing a one-piece jumpsuit that shows her muffin top so clearly, even with the large gold belt that's meant to cover it, that I feel kind of sorry for her. Some friend Brenda is not warning her about the fashion flop. I have to give it to them for trying so hard, though. For women in their early seventies or late sixties, they could easily pass for a decade younger than their years.

"How is the campaign going?" I ask Leo after I've redeemed my second drink coupon and am starting my second glass of wine.

Leo smiles, his crooked teeth tumbling over themselves in his mouth. I try not to stare, but I haven't spent this much close-up time with him before. "I think my campaign rocks," he says as if he's a sixteen-year-old and not a sixty-something-year-old man. "We are the bomb diggity bomb squad."

"The bomb...? Never mind," I say, shaking my head back and forth. I don't care that much.

"Celia's enjoying delivering brochures to all of the homes in Tucson Valley with your wife. She loves spying on everyone up close," he laughs uncomfortably.

"Pamela is my queen bee," Leo says of his wife.

Our conversation halts when everyone in the banquet hall hushes at the same time as someone new enters, someone who screams for attention in a *but I don't really want attention* kind of way. Safia, wearing her signature long, flowy skirt—this one bright orange—covers her eyes not with her tortoise-shell glasses—but with a pair of bug-eyed sunglasses. She appears to be shoeless as her rainbow-colored toes peek through with each dramatic step she takes toward us. Her red hair is held in place by a thick headband with a giant sunflower in the middle. Clearly, she's moved on from wanting to shrivel up and disappear after tinkling herself in the van. She really is a meditation expert.

"Poodles, there you are." She waves her hand dramatically across our high-top table. "I was waiting in the lobby for what seemed like hours."

"Oh, sorry about that," I say. "The...uh...the notes in the folder from Tracy said to meet directly in the banquet hall."

"Notes in a folder?"

"Yeah, didn't you get Tracy's fancy notes?" asks Leo who is eating a second cheeseburger slider. He has a dollop of ketchup on his chin, but I don't say anything.

"Do you know how much paperwork I go through in a week's time for my job as a realtor?" She chuckles gregariously. People stare. "I don't even *see* paper when I'm not at work."

"Well, you're going to have a tough time this weekend," Mario says quietly.

"Ladies and gentlemen," says a young woman from aside the bar. "Please finish your beverages and join us in the auditorium for our opening ceremonies. Our festivities will begin in ten minutes. Thank you for joining us in Phoenix!"

"See?" says Safia. Her sunflower earrings dangle from her ears dramatically as she talks. "Someone will tell me where to be. I don't need paper!"

Mario, Leo, and I shake our heads in a solidarity of fake agreement with Safia.

"This is going to be an interesting few days," Mario whispers as we walk toward the auditorium along with a thousand of our closest friends.

"That's an understatement. But once we start attending sessions, I think it will get better. It might seem *saner*."

"I hope you're right."

Yet when we enter the auditorium and are immediately given flashing necklaces with cacti and suns, I'm wondering if any hope of normalcy in Phoenix has just evaporated.

## Chapter 6

I am headed for the second-to-back row of the auditorium when I hear someone yelling my name. *"Rosi! Rosi! Down here! Mario!"* Oh no! She doesn't think I'm going to sit in the front row, does she?

"Come on, Rosi!" says Safia, as she grabs my hand and leads me to Tracy who is holding several seats, front row, center stage. Great.

"I thought you wanted *me* to hold a seat for *you*," I say when we are seated.

"Can you believe I was stood up?" Tracy asks, exasperated.

I don't have time to ask more questions—though I have many—because the curtain is dramatically opening, and thousands of senior community residents and supporters and business people break into thunderous applause. It's time to make a mental shift and embrace the opportunities to learn things that will help to grow Tucson Valley Retirement Community, my parents' home away from home, and the job I really do enjoy.

The first speaker is the president of the Arizona chapter of the Southwest Senior Living Board. She is an elegant woman with two strands of pearls and a tasteful, well-tailored pantsuit. She has that shiny gray hair that women of her age wish for, and her commanding presence and self-assured voice carry the crowd through the specifics of the year's highlights. I make a mental note to see if Adeline Vega is teaching any sessions I might want to attend.

*"And now for our guest speaker...Dr. Rafferty Smith!"*

I realize I've missed most of the introduction, lost in my thoughts about how I want to look like Adeline Vega when I grow up. Dr. Rafferty Smith, a man of many more years than my dad who sits at 70 years old, walks to the podium with a pep in his step and a lifetime of wrinkles on his face. He wears a button down short sleeve shirt that has one too many buttons open at the top and a leather vest. He has a full head of thick, gray hair and glasses that sit on his chest, attached by a chain around his neck. He talks about his new book and how retirement communities need to prepare for the future as the age of the population is skewing older, meaning that residents who reside there will be older, and activities and accommodations should

45

account for that in positive ways. He reminds all of us in the auditorium, whether a senior ourselves or working to support seniors, to remember to focus on the goal of making the last years of our lives and our residents' lives as happy and comfortable as possible. *And happy* he repeats. It's a nice sentiment, and I really enjoy listening to him speak.

"And, finally, I would be remiss if I did not bring out to the stage before I go, a fine representation of what life after 80 can look like, the joy, the fun, the vitality that exists. Please give a warm welcome to the Screamin' Seniors!"

The crowd goes wild, hooting and hollering at decibels I haven't heard since the end of the 60s Extravaganza Concert in April in Tucson Valley. Five elderly men appear on the stage, two with canes, and one being pushed in a wheelchair, but they make an entrance nonetheless in matching silver shimmering bow ties, tuxedo pants, and vests. Young people dressed in yellow t-shirts that say *STAFF* on the back run onto the stage and hand them all microphones as the music rises, and we are treated to the most entertaining rendition of "YMCA" I have ever experienced. Everyone that's able rises on their feet to participate in forming the letters with their arms.

"Oh, poodles! This is so much fun, Rosi!" Safia says as she grabs my hand to raise our Y's together in the air.

Then my fate meets my worst fear. The lead singer of the Screamin' Seniors yells something to the crowd I don't hear because Safia's still gushing in my ear, and when she raises my still clasped hand in the air, the lead singer points his cane at me. Staff in yellow shirts rush toward me and others who have raised their hands, and before I know what is happening, I'm being escorted to the stage. I look at Tracy in horror, but she just laughs as does Mario. Some friends I have!

I try to talk my way out of what is happening, but the young staffer acts as if she can't hear me. A dozen assorted attendees of the senior living conference amass around the Screamin' Seniors. I am not the youngest at 39.99999. An enthusiastic young man who looks like he's in his 20s is clapping his hands wildly in the air as the band plays in the background. Brenda, in her skintight pink dress rubs the head of the bald man in the wheelchair who squeezes her shoulder. It's disgusting.

47

"Let's give a round of applause to our volunteers!" says Dr. Rafferty Smith who has returned to the lectern.

Bald man beckons us toward him. "We're singing 'We are Family' by Sister Sledge."

"Rock on!" says twenty-something guy.

"And you've got 20 seconds to choose a prop from the box just offstage. *Twenty seconds. Go!*"

Someone steps on my foot when we disperse and handsy wheelchair guy gives my rump a little push up. When I get backstage, I walk toward the stairs that will remove me from this horrific situation, but two yellow-shirted staff members have suddenly become very serious and won't budge to let me through. I sigh, reach into the box, and grab the first thing I touch. When back on the stage, we are instructed by Dr. Smith to put on our accessories. That's when I look at my hands and see what I am holding. I want to die. I want to die right here on stage. Take me away. End my misery. I am holding an XXL size of men's bladder leakage disposable underwear. I know because the tag is staring me in the face.

"Nice choice, Rosi," Brenda smirks as she throws a lime green boa around her neck.

I have no choice. I step into the adult diaper and pull it over my pants. I hear the laughter. I know they are laughing at me. I try to step behind twenty-something guy, but he shakes his head back and forth at me with a huge grin on his face and a top hat on his head as he nudges me forward. I have to hold the underwear up as it's clearly too large. The band starts playing "We Are Family." Dr. Rafferty Smith asks the crowd to sing along. And what am I to do but wear my oversized, bladder leakage panties in front of a crowd of three thousand people and sing, "We are family..." Tracy gives me a thumbs up while Safia sways to the music as if she's listening to a different tune in her head. Jan, sitting a few rows behind the front row, is taking pictures as she sings. Just great. Social marketing is part of my job at Tucson Valley Retirement Community, but it doesn't mean *I'm* supposed to be marketing myself. And this picture *will* find its way to social media. No doubt about it.

"Let's hear it for our Screamin' Seniors backup singers!" says Dr. Smith. "Especially our friend Rosi Laruee who makes the perfect bladder leakage protection model!"

A quick glance at Brenda's face gives away the person who shared my name. I hate her. I hate her right

49

now so hard. All I want to do is go back to my room and cuddle with Barley. How do I get myself into these situations?

I rip off the underwear and throw them into the props bin, pushing past the others on my way *not back to my seat*. I exit a side door in the auditorium that leads into the hallway that takes me to the bay of elevators. My heart is beating so fast when I get onto the elevator that I have to lean against the wall to support myself while I try to slow my breaths. The elevator rings quickly on the second floor, and I decide I need some fresh air, so I push the twelfth floor button that will lead to the outside pool and deck. *I'm sorry, Barley. I need a gulp of air first* I tell myself.

The city lights illuminate the expanse of Phoenix. Another difference that I'm still adjusting to, the sun setting at 7:30 in the summer. In Illinois, it's after 8:00 before the sun sets, and when I visit my best friend Dena in Michigan, it's after 9:30 before the golden sphere falls behind the horizon. A couple of kids are splashing in the pool as Mom and Dad sit along the edge. I help myself to a glass of cucumber and mint water from the water cooler and sit on a barstool to look out over the city. My phone had told me this morning that it would be a balmy 87 degrees tonight, and I have full faith in Siri's predictions. I am thinking about whether or not I should get a wig like Brenda's to blend in unnoticed tomorrow during my sessions when I get a text message from Tracy.

*Hey! Ceremony is over. Let me know if you want to talk. Everyone loved you, Rosi. #Truth*

I sigh, not having the same faith in Tracy as I do in Siri, but I need to get back to Barley. She needs to go potty, and I need to take a long shower and go to bed. This is a work trip after all. I take the stairs down from the twelfth floor to my room on the second floor. The exercise is good for my body and soul, though I hold onto the banister. Tripping in a quiet stairwell and having to lay incapacitated on the floor as a damsel in distress until some no name Casanova comes by to save me is exactly the kind of thing that might happen tonight if I'm not careful.

I run my key over the keypad to room 221.

Barley's jumping at the other side of the door before I get inside. I reach for her leash that's sitting on the floor. "Come on, girl. Let's go." As we wait for the elevator, I go over the events of today in my head from my hike calamities with Keaton to our emotionally draining van ride to my humiliating rendition of "We Are Family" in

51

front of a crowd of thousands of strangers and a couple malintentioned co-workers.

The elevator door opens as I wait my turn to take Barley outside. Jan and Brenda exit along with Safia. All three burst into huge smiles the moment they lay eyes on me, for different reasons, of course. Safia was just purely entertained. I'm thinking maybe she needs to try that underwear after her little accident in the van, but those thoughts remain in my tired mind.

"Rosi, dear. You made this lady so happy tonight. I haven't grinned that much since I signed a deal on a three million dollar house in the Santa Rita Mountains."

"Thank you, Safia," I say sweetly.

"Quite a show!" Jan says, giggling with Brenda.

I walk past them into the elevator and don't stop Barley from licking the bottom of Brenda's leg.

I walk back onto my floor, grateful that the elevator is empty except for the hotel waiter who is delivering food to someone on my floor. The smell of fish hits my taste buds with a punch, and I wonder how much I could offer him to give *me* the dinner instead, but then he turns right while I turn left.

Barley jumps out of my arms the minute I open the door. "Geesh, girl, warn me already, okay?"

I drop my hotel key onto the dresser by the television. Barley's barking in the bathroom is giving me a headache. She can't be hungry again, can she? I look at the time. It's 8:30. I suppose a late night snack is in order for both of us. I pick up the room service menu and am trying to choose between the perch sandwich and a sensible salad when Barley starts doing zoomies around the hotel room, running from the bathroom to the bed, off the bed, spinning in circles, back to the bed, back to the bathroom, barking, and repeat. It's driving me crazy. "Point taken!" I walk into the bathroom to fill Barley's food bowl. "NOOOOOOOOOOOOOOOOOOOOOOOOOO! Not again!" I drop to my knees and cry out in frustration. Barley licks away my tears and returns to the man in the bathtub where she licks his face. He does not respond.

## Chapter 7

The Phoenix police are much more professional than Officer Dan Daniel in Tucson Valley though he tries very hard to project confidence and experience. Officer Viola Warren takes my statement at the small, round table in my room. I'm resting my feet on Barley as Officer Warren records my words while a forensics team is analyzing the crime scene in my bathroom.

"Ms. Laruee, can you tell me what you did when you discovered the male victim in your bathtub?"

I stare at a single chin hair that protrudes from her face. I wonder if I should tell her about it. I shake my head to answer my own question and sigh. Two times I have gone through this, questioned after the discovery of a dead body. I can thank Brenda for finding the body of Sherman Padowski, however. But still. Is this what happens to all women who get divorced and pivot their life plans? "Like I said, I'd just taken my dog out to pee." Barley raises her head, and I scratch under her chin. "Then I was looking at the room service menu. We only got finger food at the reception."

"The reception?"

"I'm here for the Senior Living Retirement Community Conference. Tonight was the opening session."

"Aw, that explains the, uh…the population demographic in the lobby," she says, choosing her words carefully. "But you're not a senior."

She smiles, and I'm softened by her kind face. I didn't realize how much I needed someone to talk kindly to me. I try to hold back my tears. "I'm in charge of the social media and marketing at the Tucson Valley Retirement Community Senior Center."

"Oh! Isn't that where that impersonator was killed?" she asks as she scrunches up her nose, replaying the news story phenomena that was the murder in our performing arts center.

"Yes."

"You have some sort of luck, Ms. Laruee."

"You have no idea," I say, not mentioning Salem Mansfield.

"And when you got into your bathroom…?"

"Barley was going crazy, running around and barking. I realized she was probably hungry, too, so I went to refill her dog bowl. Then she jumped onto the edge of the tub and kissed the, uh, kissed the man who's in there," I say, gesturing toward the bathroom where there is a tall, thin, handsome-ish, blonde-haired, man not much older than me who is sitting in a pool of water in my hotel bathtub with his own tie squeezed around his neck, his tongue hanging out like Barley's when she's being cute. Only there is nothing cute about this situation. And why put the man in water to begin with? Fully dressed? The addition of the bubbles was like a kick in the kidneys to a man that's already down.

"Your dog kissed our victim?"

"She did, right on the face. She's a big kisser."

"And apparently she's not very selective in whom she kisses," she laughs to herself as she doesn't make eye contact with me.

"What can I say? She's too young to have been burned by the wrong guy," I say dryly.

"That's really funny," says Officer Warren.

"Thanks?"

"Did you know the victim?" She taps her pen up and down on the table.

"I have no idea who is in my bathtub or why he is in my bathtub."

"Officer Warren?" asks a young police officer as he walks out of the bathroom holding a small rectangular card with a pair of tweezers.

"What is it, Odin?"

"This is a business card," he says, matter-of-factly.

"I can see that."

"And it has her name on it," he says, pointing to me.

"Let me see it," she says.

He walks over to the table and holds out the business card. We both read it clearly. *Rosi Laruee, Director of Marketing, Tucson Valley Retirement Community Senior Center,* with my phone number. Officer Warren looks at me.

"It's my business card. I don't know why it's in the bathroom, but I brought a bunch of cards in my briefcase for the conference. I can show you if you want to see them," I say, starting to stand up.

"The business card wasn't found in the bathroom," says Officer Odin, a young police officer with classic Hollywood looks and build.

"What?" we both say together.

57

"I mean, it *was* found in the bathroom, but it was found in our victim's shirt pocket. It was the only thing on him, no wallet, no identification."

"Why, that's impossible. I have no idea who this guy is! Why would he have *my* business card in his pocket? And why is he in *my* bathtub? And who the heck is he?"

"I have no answers, Ms. Laruee. Are you sure you don't have some information you're not telling me about?"

I take my head into my hands and flop my upper body onto the table before me. Why is this happening? Barley jumps up and licks my hand. I raise my head. "I have no information. But I am feeling kind of cursed right now."

"Is there anyone that can verify your whereabouts tonight?"

"Yes, of course. I went to the reception at 5:30 with my co-workers who are here in the hotel. And then I went to the opening ceremony." I take a deep breath. "And I imagine there's a viral video of my performance *on stage* floating around out there."

"A viral video?" asks Officer Odin. "Those are so fun!"

"This one wasn't so fun," I say quietly to myself.

"What was that?" asks Officer Warren.

"A group called the Screamin' Seniors performed at the end of the opening ceremony with volunteers from the audience. Let's just say I was *volunteered*."

Officer Odin starts laughing as he studies his phone. "Oh, yeah. I've got it right here. You're viral all right. What in the world are you wearing on your legs? It looks like a giant plastic diaper. I didn't know they made them that big!"

Clearly the young officer has never experienced geriatric incontinence. Nor have I, of course, at least not to the extent where I'd chosen to wear bladder leakage underpants intentionally. Those days are coming since I birthed a ten-pound baby back in the day.

I look away as Officer Warren watches the video. "You don't look very comfortable on that stage, Ms. Laruee."

"I was not," I say softly.

"And when this, uh, little show, was over, did you come straight back to your room?"

"No. I needed air, so I took the elevator to the top floor and hung out by the pool."

"And was there anyone who can corroborate this story?" Her tone has turned serious again.

"Yeah, there was a family there, a couple and their kids. But I don't know who they are. There are thousands of people in this hotel right now. I can assure you that the video cameras on the elevator and the roof will account for my whereabouts."

Officer Warren nods her head and gestures to Officer Odin to make the call for the videos. "And then you came to your room?"

"I did, but I didn't come into the room very far."

"Go on," she says, as I roll my eyes, irritated that I'm being interrogated as if I am the subject of this investigation.

"Barley hadn't been let out for a long time." She lifts her head at the sound of her name and growls as if to say, *I was sleeping. Leave me alone.* I pet her to let her know I'm not moving anytime soon at the rate this interview is going. "I had left her leash inside the door, right where it is right now. I point to the floor by the front door where the leash and poop bags are sitting. "I took her out to pee. The hotel has a dog area."

"And *then* you found the body when you returned."

"No."

Officer Warren throws down her pen. "No?"

"I sat on the bed and looked at the room service menu as I *already told you!* Then Barley..." I say, covering her ears, "found the body by barking and acting all crazy. And then I called 911. And here we are. Can you please tell me who is in my bathtub?"

A knock on the door startles us all. "That's probably management. I asked for the video," says Officer Odin who opens the door.

"Oh my goodness, Rosi! Are you okay? What's going on?" Tracy walks into the room followed by Safia. Brenda and Jan form the caboose of the new train of people.

"Who are these people?" Officer Warren asks as she stands up, clearly irritated by their interruption.

"My team from Tucson Valley."

"Rosi? What's going on?" demands Brenda who has changed into a terry cloth track suit with her initials embroidered on the breast. But, of course, she's still wearing a face full of makeup.

I look at Officer Warren and telepathically will her to explain this most unfortunate situation.

"Ladies, this room is a crime scene. I need you to step outside, please."

"A crime scene?" asks Safia. Her wrinkles deepen with concern.

"Rosi?" asks Tracy.

I sigh. "Someone deposited a dead body in my bathtub," I say dryly as it's become quite normal for dead bodies to drop out of the sky when I'm nearby.

"WHAT?" shrieks Jan. "AGAIN?"

Officer Odin escorts everyone back toward the door. They have no choice but to leave.

"Rosi, call me!" I hear Tracy shout from the hallway.

Officer Odin walks back into the room with the hotel manager, a stern man with a handlebar mustache that's as wide as his full face. "Mr. Quinta has the video footage downloaded," he says with too much pep in his voice.

"I've examined the video footage for this floor as well as the elevator," Mr. Quinta says with a bass toned voice that would give James Earl Jones a run for his money.

"Thank you, but we'll do our own investigation now," Officer Warren says. "We will let you know if we have any further questions. I am sure that we will."

"Yes, but I need to let you know that no one else has been in this room but Ms. Laruee. No one else is seen coming in or out of the room except for that cute dog," he says, pointing toward Barley and waving as if Barley will raise her paw back in a greeting.

"Wait. Do you mean to suggest that the guy in my bathtub just magically appeared?" I ask in frustration. *"He's not even in the video footage?"*

"He did not enter your room through the hallway."

"Is this room connected to the next room?" asks Officer Warren.

"It is," Mr. Quinta says. "There," he points to the door behind the closet. "It adjoins to the next room, though it's locked on both sides. Room service and the cleaning staff are the only people who have been in that room, all employees."

"And who are the registered guests in the adjoining room?" asks Officer Warren who is pursing her lips together as if she's kissing the air.

"Jan, Brenda, and Safia."

"Who?" asks Officer Warren.

"The women who were just in the room. They came with me."

63

"Oh. Do you think they might know this gentleman?"

"I have no idea."

Officer Warren sighs. "Ugh. Go get them," she says to Office Odin.

"Why?"

"Well, it's most unorthodox, but we have a dead body in a bathtub in a hotel room that no one can identify. If there's any chance that the only other room connected to this one has guests that may have an association with this man, we have to ask them."

"It's not going to go well," I say quietly to myself. "Not well at all."

Officer Odin walks back into the hotel room with Brenda, Jan, and Safia. Safia holds a paper fan which she is waving wildly back and forth in front of her face as if she's having a hot flash. She's still wearing a long skirt, though more casual than the one she'd worn to the opening ceremony. I wonder if her legs have ever seen the light of day. I imagine two pasty white Elmer's Glue sticks for legs under that skirt. Jan looks horrified to be back in my room as she'd clearly been caught off guard with a face full of overnight moisturizer lathered in snowy white upon her face. I hide my laughter behind my hand. Barley hops up and runs toward Jan where he jumps on her leg and barks until Officer Odin grabs her by the collar and brings her back to me.

"Why on Earth do you think we can help here?" demands Brenda.

"Hello. I am Officer Warren. Ladies, your room adjoins a crime scene with a door that opens onto this one. We need to identify a man who has lost his life here tonight, and if his presence here is at all related to Ms. Laruee or any of you, we need to know that."

"Any of *us?* Are you crazy?" asks Brenda. "I want you to know that I am a mayoral candidate. I am in the government! The audacity you have to suggest that I have something to do with a dead body in Rosi's room is outrageous!"

Officer Warren ignores Brenda completely. "Ma'am, what's your name?" she asks Safia gently as she looks like she's trying to prevent a panic attack by taking slow, deep breaths. Poor thing. I bet this is the first murdered body she's seen. We all have to start somewhere.

"Safia Devereaux," she says quietly.

"Like Blanche Devereaux on the Golden Girls?" Officer Odin asks. "My mom loved that show!"

*Didn't everyone's mom* I want to say. If you only knew *my* full name. Safia doesn't answer, though.

"All I need from you ladies is to take a peek at our victim. Don't worry. There's no blood. Look at the face and tell us if you recognize him. Then you are free to go."

"Oh, my God in heaven above!" Brenda makes the sign of the cross over her heart and marches into the bathroom only to return seconds later. "I do not know him." She slams the hotel door behind her, leaving Safia and Jan looking at each other to will the other to go first.

After a few moments of uncomfortable staring, Jan walks slowly into the bathroom. "Oh my!" And then she runs out of the room with her hand over her mouth. "I don't...I don't know him. Goodbye."

Safia looks so pitiful. She's begun talking to herself. "You can do this, Safia. You can do this. You can do this."

I feel so sorry for her. I tie Barley's leash to my chair leg and join Safia outside the bathroom. I offer her my hand. "I'll go with you, Safia. It will be quick. Just a small look, okay?"

She looks up at me, for the first time seeming to register that there are other people in the room. She nods her head. We walk into the bathroom. The bubbles are almost gone. Safia freezes for a moment as she looks at the body, squeezing my hand so tightly, I think she might break my finger. As expected, she does not know the victim, either. Officer Odin takes her back to her room.

"Are you satisfied that none of us have anything to do with this craziness?" I ask.

"We will be in touch, Ms. Laruee. Mr. Quinta, thank you for your help. The coroner will be here momentarily to remove the body, and our crime scene team is almost finished."

"Good. Please let me know if I can be of any further assistance." He turns to go.

"Wait! Wait! You don't expect me to *stay in this room?* There's been a murder here! Hello? What about *me?*"

Mr. Quinta looks at me. "Ms. Laruee, you know about the conference. Why, every room is full. What am I to do about that?" He holds up his hands. Not his problem.

"You can't be serious? I can't stay here!"

"Your co-workers may have space, but I have no more rooms. I am sorry. That's just the way it is. But you sure do have a cute dog."

"That's just the way it is," I repeat just as sarcastically as I intended it to sound.

I pack the few things I'd removed from my luggage, text Tracy to expect me, grab Barley's things and leash, and walk toward the door.

"Watch yourself, Ms. Laruee," says Officer Warren. "This might have been some kind of warning meant for you."

"For me?" I ask.

"You never know. Be careful."

## Chapter 8

Tracy had been so sweet last night. She'd even gone so far as to barricade her room by pushing a chair under the door handle, assuring the chain was locked, and purchasing pepper spray at the local pharmacy across the street from the hotel. I hadn't slept more than a couple of hours though. Keaton had actually talked to me until I fell asleep, though I didn't stay asleep for very long. I'd put my AirPods in and let him read to me from his *Landscape Weekly Magazine* until I'd drifted off.

This morning it's back to work. Conference sessions to attend. Things to learn. Things to forget. But first I have another meeting with Officer Warren. Hers was the first text I'd seen this morning.

"Rosi, I insist you take this pepper spray," says Tracy. "No one knows what is happening. No one knows if you are in any kind of danger. *Please.* Your mother would never forgive me if I let something happen to you."

"Okay, thanks. I'll take the pepper spray if you promise me that you won't mention any of this to my mother. She doesn't need to worry."

Tracy looks up at the ceiling and taps her foot up and down.

"Tracy! You didn't tell Mom, did you?"

"I didn't! I promise. But, I…"

"You, did *what?*"

"I texted her that I had something really important to tell her."

"Then you need to come up with something else exciting to tell her. Do you promise?"

"Yes, fine. I promise. It's just that…"

"What? Spit it out."

"Well, we pinky swore that we'd never lie to each other. It's kind of a tap-dance partner pledge we made the first time we had to perform during class on the mini stage."

I shake my head, exasperated by the woman who is both like an older sister to me and a younger sister to my mother. "Find something else *interesting* to tell her," I say through gritted teeth, grabbing the container of pepper spray and throwing it in my purse.

Officer Warren stands up and waves me over when I walk into the hotel's coffee shop. "Good morning, Rosi.

How was the rest of your evening?" she asks with a note of empathy in her voice that's welcomed.

"Challenging."

She nods her head. "I can imagine. I wanted to give you some basic information. The hotel has agreed to keep the murder in your bathtub quiet—for now. There are thousands of people here for the Senior Living Retirement Community Conference, as you know. It would be financially unfortunate for the hotel and the conference organizers if word were to get out about what happened in room 221."

"I don't plan on beginning any conversations today about the dead man in my bathtub. Don't worry about me. But there are a couple of big gossips in the room adjoining room 221."

"I've sent Officer Odin to speak with them. And the president of the Arizona chapter of the Southwest Senior Living Board, Adeline Vega, has been notified. Should any information leak, she's prepared with a statement to distance the conference from what's happened."

"Do you think there's a connection between this conference and that guy in my tub?" I accept a piping hot cup of coffee from the waitress.

"Well, the only bit of information we have is your business card in his shirt pocket, so it's a possibility."

"I can assure you that I have no idea who that man was!" I can feel the heat rising up my face.

"Don't worry, Rosi. No one suspects your involvement. Quite the contrary. Officer Odin had a very long discussion with his cousin last night who vouched every which way for you in the most positive way possible."

"His cousin?"

"Yes, didn't he tell you?"

"Officer Odin didn't tell me anything," I say, spying Leo and Mario speaking with Jan and Brenda in the lobby outside of the café. News will spread. It will spread fast. I sigh.

"Officer Dan Daniel in Tucson Valley is Officer Odin's first cousin. Their moms are sisters. He describes their relationship as more like brothers than cousins."

"Oh, okay. That's good, I guess." I add another sugar pack to my coffee mug.

"But watch your back. There's going to be increased police presence here. Don't hesitate to reach out if you see something or if you need anything."

"Thank you." I check my watch. "I need to get to my first session."

"Have a good day, Ms. Laruee. The station will pick up the check."

"Thanks."

I am about to enter the room for my first session, *Unlocking the Potential of Your Social Media Marketing,* when Mario stops me with a huge hug that catches me so off guard that we tumble into the wall where I hit my head on a giant painting of a cactus. "Ouch!"

"Rosi! I'm so sorry! I've been so worried about you ever since I talked to Jan and Brenda this morning. You should have called me last night. Leo and I could have helped."

"Thanks, Mario," I say, rubbing the top of my head. "There's nothing you could have done. Barley and I stayed with Tracy. The police want to keep it quiet. The media isn't being notified, so no matter the way Jan or Brenda were acting, we're supposed to keep this hush hush."

"I understand. I won't say a word. I haven't even told Celia, though she's not the gossip type. Do you need anything?" His smile is so sincere I can't even be angry about the knot forming on the top of my head.

"I need today to be problem free."

Mario laughs. "Well, I can't promise that, but it should be fun. Tonight's wild west party should put a pep in your step."

"Yee-haw," I say, unenthusiastically.

"You'll see, Cowgirl Rosi. It will be a rip roarin' good time! You'd better get to your session. I'm headed to *Senior Center Safety and Security*. Try saying that ten times!"

"Have an educational day, Mario. I'll see you tonight."

I open the door to my session, trying to slip into a back row seat, but the back row is full. And the second to back row and the third to back row and so on. I have to excuse myself to find a seat in the middle of the fourth row. A few giggles float in the air, but I don't realize they are directed my way until I am seated and look up at the speaker. A man in his 30s or 40s is standing still, a cocky swagger on his hips as he moves from side to side. He holds a clicker in his hand. Behind him, on a large screen, a video has been paused. And there I am, in extra, extra large adult diapers pulled over my pants with the TikTok logo in the corner.

"What a delight to have the subject of our viral social media grace us with her presence. Let's give her a rousing applause!"

The crowd erupts in applause with a few hoots and hollers for effect as I sink lower into my chair. I wish I could evaporate.

"Miss, would you care to share any words?" Mr. Speaker holds his microphone out in my direction.

I shake my head no.

"Are you sure? This may be your fifteen minutes of fame, and surely you don't want to miss this opportunity to talk to your fans."

I look up and realize that there are multiple camera phones held up recording my reaction. I don't dare move.

"Carry on, please."

He waits for what seems like five minutes before realizing that I am not budging. "So, as I was saying, this video is an example of how fast social media can spread. Since we began ten minutes ago, this video has had 15,000 more views making the total at 345,000!"

*Oh my God in heaven. Please, please make this stop,* I pray though I'm not sure God is working today.

"What your goal should be within your own retirement communities, ladies and gentlemen, is to look for opportunities to highlight the good—the fun that your community offers—and to highlight your residents and programs in engaging videos. We are going to cover hashtags, influencers…"

Blah. Blah. Blah. If it were easy to make a quiet exit, I'd be gone. Instead, I pull out my phone and silently text with Keaton, my saving grace.

*Imagine he's dressed in a chicken suit doing the chicken dance.*

Try harder. Not working.

*Okay. Imagine him dressed in his birthday suit. You said he was young.*

Ooh! Gross!

*Guess I'm glad that was your reaction. LOL*

It's almost over. Thanks.

*Send pics in your cowboy hat tonight.*

Not likely.

*Come on! I stayed awake all night worrying about you. It's the least you can do.*

I'll consider it. Bye.

Heart emoji

While everyone is clapping for the speaker, I stand up and leave the room before anyone can whip their phone out again.

I check my schedule in the file folder Tracy had provided for my next session: *Themed Lunches*. I decide that I'll read through the notes online when they are posted tonight. I want to blend in, not stand out. I won't take that chance again, at least not before lunch. I walk toward the exhibit hall where I hope to fill up on free pens, rulers, notepads, and cheap plastic water bottles; and if I can acquire a collection of wrapped chocolate candy bars, I'll call it a successful morning.

I do value my job and the worth I can offer the residents of Tucson Valley. I know that they deserve for me to get *something* positive out of this conference to enrich their lives, so I pay attention to the booths that seem important and take business cards when I'm interested in a service or a product. The seatback supports for theater seating seem like a good idea. Many of our guests at the performing arts center complain about the seats being hard on their backs, so I talk to the representative from the Back

It Up Company and take a brochure. I check my schedule and realize it's almost time for lunch. I text Tracy to ask her to save me a spot at her table.

"Rosi?"

I turn around to the familiar voice that belongs to my former karaoke partner, the partner who'd embarrassed me in front of a crowd of people at the senior center bar when we'd sung "Islands in the Stream," my Dolly Parton to his Kenny Rogers. "What are you doing here?" we say at the same time. We gawk at each other, both in complete surprise.

Allen, the same Allen who happens to be Jan Jinkins's nephew, points to the display for his company, Vermin Be Gone, an exterminator business based out of Nevada. "My company has gone regional, Rosi. We've contracted with over five retirement communities in the Southwest, and we are hoping to double those contracts by the end of the year."

"Cool." I can't think of anything more interesting to say.

"Tracy Lake came by this morning. She's signing with our services for Tucson Valley. You'll probably be seeing me around."

"Okay, Allen. Good luck with everything."

"Here. Take an inflatable rat. Your dog will like it."

Allen thrusts a deflated rodent into my hands. I slip it into my bag. "Thanks."

"Hey! How are your parents?"

I consider the man before me, jet black, tightly curled hair slicked back kind of like he'd done when we'd sung together the night of the '80s party at the senior bar, though he'd missed the mark on the decade completely. He's wearing large-framed glasses. They must be new as I don't remember them, but I appreciate the thoughtful question. "Mom and Dad are in Branson, Missouri, this weekend. They're attending a dinner theater murder mystery."

"That's awesome. Sounds like they are living their best lives."

"I think they are. Thanks." I give a little wave goodbye, but Allen isn't done.

"I saw your video!" A laugh much deeper than one would expect from his scrawny body falls out of his mouth. "You looked ridiculous."

He smiles with so much satisfaction that I can't give him anything else to be gleeful over. "Glad you enjoyed it,"

79

I say, walking away with a fake smile plastered on my face. What a jerk.

## Chapter 9

Tracy waves me over to her table after I've waded through the buffet line and gotten my grilled chicken, mashed potatoes, and asparagus. I know it's an unpopular opinion, but I've always found convention food to be delightful. The best taco bar I've ever seen was at a journalist convention I'd attended in Chicago. From what I've observed today, many attendees like this food, too. The guy in front of me took two full helpings of potatoes.

"Hey, Rosi! How are you doing? I hope you've had some awesome sessions to take your mind off of—things." Tracy pats the open chair next to her.

I spare Tracy the details of my social media session as well as the fact that I skipped the second one and instead focus on my unexpected meeting with Allen.

"Ugh! I was hoping you could avoid him. I imagine he told you about the new contract I signed with his company on behalf of Tucson Valley."

"He did."

"You know I had to do that, right? Because of Jan?"

I nod my head. "I know. Political move. How have your sessions been?" I ask as I spoon a large helping of mashed potatoes into my mouth.

"Fantastic! Well, the rules and regulations meeting was dry as usual, but I got a lot of great ideas at the tech session."

I raise my eyebrows in surprise. "The great file-folders-loving Tracy Lake is thinking of updating the technology at the senior center?"

She laughs. "Baby steps. I can't lose my file folders just yet, but let's say I am open to technology updates. I don't like change, but the more I learn, the more I understand."

"That's good, Tracy. Let me know how I can help."

"I will. Plus, I have a super exciting meeting at 5:45 today that I haven't told anyone about! The meeting was supposed to happen last night, but it fell through. I'm so glad we could reschedule." She's smiling so expectantly that her cheeks look like they might pop from excitement.

I cut off a piece of chicken and wait for her to continue, but that's when Safia sits down next to me. "Ladies, what a day it's been. I'm exhausted with knowledge." She takes such a long drink of her ice water

I'm not sure we will have time to talk before we have to leave for our afternoon sessions. "Sorry about that. I was parched!"

"I am so glad you are having a good day, Safia," says Tracy. "What sessions have you attended?"

I know that Tracy has all the answers. She created the file folders after all, but I think she truly enjoys hearing the excitement from our learning. Her heart belongs to Tucson Valley Retirement Community.

"Well, in *How to Drive Occupancy* I was able to share my techniques for closing a sale," she says, so proud of herself that I feel like I should pull a gold sticker out of my purse and slap it on her paisley shirt that matches the identical print on her flowy skirt.

"You were able to share?" Tracy asks, excited.

"I was. And everyone learned so much from *me!*"

"Did you learn anything from the speaker?" I ask the obvious question.

Safia dismisses me with a frowny face. "I've been in the real estate business for thirty years. Do you really think there is anything that I don't already know?"

"Got it," I say. If there is one area in life that Safia exudes arrogance over, it's her love for real estate. I'm more

83

amused than annoyed by her overconfidence. She is, in fact, an amazing realtor. "I need to run back to my room and let Barley out," I say as I see Jan and Brenda walking toward our table. "I'll meet you all for drinks at 5:00. Have a great afternoon everyone!"

I only glance at Jan and Brenda as I pass by. Jan is wearing another one-piece jumpsuit with a blazer. Should *I* step in and tell her that Brenda is sabotaging her fashion choices by not telling her friend that the jumpsuit style does her no favors? I choose to ignore them both instead. I suppose if you are entering your seventies, you can wear whatever the heck you want to wear. I do stop to acknowledge Mario and Leo, though, who are filling up at the dessert table that I'd missed. "I hope you gentlemen are behaving yourselves," I tease.

"Having a grand time, Rosi," says Leo. "Picking up some tips for my mayoral campaign."

"And these desserts are to die for," says Mario. "How are you?" Mario's words are so full of concern like that special uncle who knows your thoughts before you do.

"I'm okay." I glance around me. Most people are absorbed in their lunches and conversations, not focusing on the senior diaper wearer. Clearly the word about the murder in the hotel has been contained. "I've got to run up and check on Barley. I'll see you guys in the bar later!"

"And don't forget the seniors' stampede!" says Leo. "I've got my chaps ready to go!"

"Can't wait," I lie as I turn to weave my way through the banquet hall.

I nearly collide with a man who turns the corner in my floor hallway so quickly that both of have to react fast. "Sorry!" I say though it's not me who's walking like a madman. Why do I always feel the need to apologize first?

The man looks startled when he looks up. "Okay," is all he says as he continues walking. But then he stops before the elevator and turns around. "Hey!" he yells.

"Excuse me?"

"You're that lady," he says.

Oh great. Here we go again. Plastic diapers.

"The bathtub lady."

I suck in my breath and peer closer at the lightly balding man before me, tufts of thin, gray hair above his ears. He's wearing jogging pants and an Arizona State sweatshirt. A tattoo of a cactus covers the entire right side of his neck. "Excuse me?" I repeat.

"That dead guy. You're the one cops think killed that guy in your tub. Why aren't you in jail?"

I walk toward him as the elevator dings for the second floor. A couple gets out and stare at us as they pass by. "How do you know about that?" I demand, throwing my hands on my hips to match my attitude.

"I, uh, I, everyone knows. It's all over," he says, standing up straighter as if he can assert his power through a few extra inches.

"That's a lie. No one knows but those that *have to know* about what happened last night. And, for the record, I didn't kill anyone." I squint my eyes and dare him to call me a liar.

"Oh, well, maybe I was wrong. I'm…I need to go." He turns around and pushes the elevator button again.

Just because he's turned his back on me doesn't mean he can walk away that simply. I move in front of the elevator and push him in the chest. "Tell me how you learned about the bathtub *incident*. Tell me how you found out. Who are you? What's your name?"

The elevator door dings, but I throw out my hands so he can't get past me. A young woman on the elevator has to duck under my arms to exit. She gives me a horrified look and hurries away.

"Get out of my way," he growls.

"Tell me who you are."

He looks like a mouse corned by the cat. Then he takes off, running down the hallway toward the exit that will take him to the stairs and the exit out of the hotel. I know because that's my exit door to take Barley potty. What is going on? I want to scream. I want to sleep. I want to go home. Instead, I go back to my room where Barley greets me with a series of sloppy kisses that soften my worried mind. And that's when I realize that maybe I wasn't talking to someone who simply found out about the guy in my bathtub but the actual man who killed him. The thought makes me want to vomit. And I seriously question my judgment. I pick up my phone to call Officer Warren.

## Chapter 10

I'm surprised to see Adeline Vega as the listed speaker for one of the sessions on the list. I decide to skip my regularly scheduled class about holiday events to attend her session on *The Brain and Music*. Bob Horace's elderly father had attended our Tucson Valley Orchestra Summer Series show in July. At almost 100 years old, he'd travelled via a wheelchair that Karen and Bob lovingly took turns pushing down the long hallway into the auditorium. I'd made sure there would be accessible seating for them all in the front row. Bob was proud to introduce me to his dad. Lawrence Horace had been a train engineer with the Union Pacific Railroad for forty years and married to his high school sweetheart for seventy years when she'd died from heart problems ten years ago. Bob had said that Lawrence had nearly died of a broken heart himself, but he'd rallied and even lived in the Tucson Valley Retirement Community for some time before going to stay in a more specialized treatment facility five years ago. His memory had faded quickly, but can you hold that against someone who's lived for nearly a century?

After the show, I'd been saying my goodbyes when the elder Mr. Horace pulled on the sleeve of my shirt. I bent down to hear his frail voice. I'll never forget what he said. He said, *"Pretty lady, I don't know my own name right now, and I bet I forgot to wipe my ass this morning, but that music takes me back to the times with my beautiful Eloise, and we danced and embraced together in my mind for the last who the heck knows how long we've been here. And that, pretty lady, is the beauty of the mind."*

Bob had been horrified that he'd spoken to me like that, but I'd been heartened and mesmerized. And any chance I can get to learn about the mind and how it changes as we age and how it can be best harnessed for our elder residents, sign me up. This time I sit in the back row. Few people pay me any attention. These attendees seem more serious than the social media crowd. I am grateful.

Adeline Vega elaborates on her resume which is so much more than being the president of the Arizona chapter of the Southwest Senior Living Board. She'd received her master's degree in gerontology, studying health and aging. She's likely in her 60s now, and I wonder as she ages if she's happy or irritated that she's become the age of the people she's studied her whole life. I still want to be her when I grow up, though, or at least I want to look like her.

89

Today, she wears a tailored navy blue pantsuit with a white blouse and a bright yellow necklace that matches her bracelet. Her heels must be at least three inches. I can't even keep upright in two-inch wedges.

"Can I sit there?" a gruff voice asks.

I look up to see Jan standing next to my chair. She wears a frown that matches her ugly brown blazer. "Uh, sure." I move my knees to the side so that she can pass by.

Adeline Vega knows how to capture a crowd. Her examples of the power of music on the mind for the memory-challenged leaves many a participant dabbing their eyes. I'm most surprised, however, to see Jan taking a tissue from her purse.

After the presentation has ended, I can see Jan still wiping the corners of her eyes in my peripheral vision. I suck up my pride and speak first before we separate. "Jan, are you okay?" I ask softly.

She looks up with a start as if she'd forgotten that she was sitting next to me. She wrinkles up her face. I imagine something mean is about to fly out of her mouth, but instead her face contorts in pain, deeply wrinkling every wrinkle that hasn't been medically removed. Her lip quivers.

"Oh, Jan. I'm sorry. I...I...did Adeline bring up a painful memory?" She bites her lip. I hand her a fresh tissue from my purse.

"Thanks." She uses the tissue to blow her nose.

"My mother."

"...had memory problems?" I ask after she doesn't finish the sentence.

She nods her head.

"That must have been really hard on all of you."

"It was." She looks at her watch. "I need to meet Brenda at the *Building Better HOA Boards* session," she says.

"I hope you have a nice afternoon."

She looks at me with surprise.

"I really do mean it, Jan. I'm not the terrible person that you think I am."

"Nor am I. I'll see you for drinks, Rosi."

Before she leaves the room, she turns around and comes back to me. She pauses. For a minute, I don't know if she is going to hug me or hit me. "Thank you," she says simply. Then she walks out of the room. Perhaps we've turned over a new leaf.

"Ms. Laruee?"

I am startled to see Adeline Vega standing next to the door. "Hello," I say, wondering how she knows my name. *Ahh, the video,* I presume, as someone had outed my name in the comments as well as on the stage.

"Hello. May I have a word with you? Privately?"

I notice her perfectly manicured nails painted a pale pink color that matches her lipstick. "Uh, sure. I have a few minutes before my next session." I follow her to the side of the room that is starting to fill up as the new speaker is preparing to speak. He's got props, too. Arches of balloon decorations are being carried into the room.

"How are you doing, dear?"

"Well, the video was humiliating, but the beauty of social media is that there will be another viral video coming along to replace mine," I laugh uneasily.

She looks confused but catches on quickly. "Oh, no, no, no! That's not what I was talking about although I *am* happy that you've recovered from Rafferty Smith's disastrous act."

I'm happy for her support, but I hadn't realized there'd been people in the audience who weren't entertained by my shenanigans. "What I meant was, how are you doing after the whole man in your bathtub circumstance?" she asks quietly yet so directly that I'm caught off guard.

"Oh! I didn't realize...oh, Officer Warren told you because you're the president, right?" I say more to myself that to Adeline.

"Yes. Don't worry. Only pertinent staff know anything about the unfortunate situation."

"I'm fine. I am kind of getting used to dead bodies." I throw my hand over my mouth the minute the words have escaped past my lips. "That sounded bad. Sorry, I've had some unfort—"

Adeline puts her hand on my arm. "I know about your past, Ms. Laruee. You've had a rough year," she smiles sweetly.

"You have no idea." I glance at the clock on the wall behind Adeline's head. "I need to get to my next session if you don't mind. I really did enjoy your presentation."

"Of course. Watch yourself. It's a scary world out there."

"Uh-huh," I say as I scrunch up my face and walk away.

I enter the other side of the exhibition hall that is blocked off by partition walls. My final session of the day is more of an entertainment showcase. Acts from all over the country are vying for bookings at the various retirement communities that are represented here. It will be a nice break to walk around and talk to entertainers, watch their videos on their video screens, or to even witness live acts. The dancing dogs I'd heard all about from Mario after I started my job at the performing arts center are putting on a display, standing on their back feet in a synchronized dance to Beyonce's "All the Single Ladies." I'm not sure if Mario would forgive me if I hired them back to perform after the hours he'd spent buffing the scratch marks on the stage floor.

I'm amused by the Betty White and Bea Arthur-playing actresses from the Golden Girls' Musical. Mom would flip out if I booked them for Tucson Valley. I take a brochure as well as a sticker with their pictures for Mom.

"Rosi Laruee?"

I hear my name called for the second time today in the exhibit hall. A small man stands behind a sign that masks his appearance, but I'd recognize that voice anywhere. "Kenny!" I envelope the Tommy Davis Jr.

impersonator who'd been a star impersonator in our Sizzlin' '60s Summer Extravaganza Concert. What a great night it had been, too—until Sherman Padowski was murdered. "What are you doing here?"

He's wearing a metallic purple vest that sparkles under the light of the hall. He points to the sign behind him. I'm working on a one-man show," he says proudly. I've created a nice playlist of songs that will really highlight my range, Rosi. Plus, I'm passing out brochures for performances with Clyde, too."

"Aww, that's awesome, Kenny. It's nice to know that Filly Sinclair and Tommy Davis Jr. will be back together again. Your solo show sounds great, too. I'd be happy to put a good word in for you with other retirement communities. You were real professionals."

"That's great, Rosi. Say, guess what? I've got a roommate now, and I'm able to pay my own rent. That show in Tucson Valley was a real catalyst for positive change for me. I can't thank you enough."

"Kenny, the thanks go to you and the other performers. It was a great night."

"Mostly."

"Mostly," I say, trying to shake Sherman Padowski from my mind. "And you'll come back in the fall, right? When we have the benefit concert for the men and women's shelters in the Tucson Valley area?"

"It will be my pleasure. They took care of me when I needed it most." A woman with a badge that says *Green Grounds Retirement Community* picks up a brochure and pauses to watch a video of Kenny singing.

"You won't be disappointed, miss," I say. "This guy's the real deal."

Kenny winks at me before I turn to walk away. I have my eye on the acrobatic act down the aisle.

## Chapter 11

It's freezing in the exhibit hall, so I decide to grab Barley for a walk on the roof and to dip my toes into the pool. Barley meets me at the door. She's clearly tired of this place, too. "I know, girl. We'll be going home tomorrow. One more day. Then we can both see Keaton again." I ruffle her fur as she sits obediently for her leash to be attached to her collar.

The hotel manager, Mr. Quinta, is hosing down the deck on the roof when Barley and I enter from the hallway. "There's my favorite dog," he says, stopping to let Barley drink from the hose.

"Hello, Mr. Quinta. Sure is a hot one up here."

"That it is. Won't take long to burn that skin. Be careful, Rosi."

There are several children splashing in the pool as well as sunbathers sitting under umbrellas trying to keep comfortable if that's something that's even possible in 100 degree temperatures. There is a small fake turf area for dogs on the roof. This hotel really has their act together when it comes to the support of dog owners, but I realize I've made a mistake. There is no way Barley can walk around this concrete. Her poor feet would suffer. Instead, I pick her up and carry her to an empty chair. I hope that nobody pulls out their camera to record my less than graceful wrangling of my forty pound puppy, but I'd do just about anything for her. As soon as she's on a chair under an umbrella, I tie her leash to the side table and sit on the pool deck farthest from the kids to soak my legs in the water. Today I'd worn a simple skirt to the meetings, so I hike it up to keep it from getting wet. I don't realize I'm being spoken to until someone nearby kicks their legs in the water.

"You come here often?" he repeats.

"Oh, sorry. I didn't realize...Dr. Smith?" I shade my eyes with my hand and squint at the man who'd humiliated me in front of thousands of people.

"Yes, you remember," he smiles kindly, deep wrinkles prominent as his lips curl up.

"How could I forget?" I mumble.

"You know, I've never had anyone choose the incontinence underwear. That was very brave of you. I'd only added them to the prop box as a lark."

"Oh. It wasn't a conscious decision."

He nods his head silently for a moment. "I figured that after I saw your face on stage."

"And on video, perhaps? As viewed by hundreds of thousands of people now?" I stick my arms into the pool to cool off and wonder if I'm getting a sunburn.

"I think social media can bring a lot of joy to people."

"Or harm," I say sarcastically.

"But you brought more joy than harm to people in that auditorium, Rosi. And to all of the people that viewed your performance online. And, from what I've been told, the Screamin' Seniors are having to field so many calls and emails inquiring about bookings that they've had to bring on an agent."

"Glad I could help," I say, rolling my eyes. I glance back at Barley who is sleeping under the umbrella.

"I *am* sorry that you were hurt, though."

I squint in his direction again. Genuineness is written all over his face, and even though I want to stay mad at this man, I cannot. "Thank you. I appreciate it. I need to get my dog some water, and I'm meeting my co-workers for drinks before the big stampede western shindig thing." I twirl my finger in the air in a la-di-da gesture.

Barley has gained five pounds in sweat in the twenty minutes I've been on the roof. I pick her up and carry her into the hallway where we will take the elevator back to our floor, and I will have to change my clothes. Sweaty dog equals stinky dog. While I am waiting for the elevator and Barley is licking the tops of my toes through my sandals, I wonder why Dr. Smith remembered my name.

The hotel bar is *the* place to be at 5:00 on a Saturday during a senior center convention. Sales execs and marketing teams fill the high top tables and the booths. The drinks flow and various platters of appetizers are passed around. There's a genial atmosphere. The last of the hard work is nearly done. Party tonight, an early morning session, and everyone will drive or fly back to their lives tomorrow. A fair share of seniors clutter the bar, too. There are senior representatives like Jan and Brenda, people invested enough in their own demographic to try to learn something positive to take back to their communities. I look for Kenny, but I don't see him. I *do* see my team, though. Tracy is sitting between Leo and Mario in a corner booth. Brenda sits aside Leo, which must be testy for the opposing mayoral candidates. Jan and Safia sit in chairs at the table. There is one seat left between them.

"Oh, poodles, Rosi! There you are, my dear!" says Safia warmly.

"Great! Now my remarkable team is complete," says Tracy as she lifts her wine glass.

"To Tucson Valley Retirement Community!" says Mario.

"To Tucson Valley!" everyone says, clinking glasses. I raise an imaginary glass in the air as the waitress walks my direction to take my order. I notice that Brenda is drinking the hardest liquor, the rest of the table drinking wine or beer.

When I'm given my order of white wine, Leo leads the table in another round of toasts. "Cheers to Tucson Valley!" he says.

"To us!"

"Cheers!"

"Oh, good gracious guacamole. Can we *stop* with the cheers?" asks Brenda, her normally biting attitude in particular overdrive. With hair hanging in her eyes and mascara smudged underneath them, Brenda looks awry.

"What's the matter, dear?" asks Safia, putting her hand on top of Brenda's which she pulls away so hard that Leo has to catch his beer bottle from rolling off the table.

Jan looks away from everyone at the table. She looks poised to run out of the room altogether. I look from Brenda to Jan and wonder if there's trouble in paradise. Perhaps sharing a hotel room is proving *too* much together time.

"I would like to commend you all for giving up your personal time to learn and to grow and to bring about new ideas that will energize and support our wonderful population. Our residents are quite lucky to be represented by all of you," says Tracy.

I think she's about to offer another toast, but she doesn't.

"I have some *very* exciting news that I can't share quite yet, but trust me, it is *big!*" She claps her hands together in excitement like Hudson when he sees his favorite cartoon characters dance across the screen.

I notice Officer Odin walking through the crowds of people. I'd seen him a few times throughout the day, part of the extra police presence, I guess, but now he seems headed for our table. I take another drink of wine and wait.

"Excuse me," he says, running a hand through his perfectly layered blonde hair. He looks more like a movie star than a police officer. "I, uh, I have a message for Rosi, I mean, for Ms. Laruee—a private message."

"Certainly, Officer," says Safia. "Come on, dear. Meet with the handsome young man." I take a deep breath and yet another drink.

I follow Officer Odin out of the bar and into the lobby. "Sorry about that," he says, laughing uneasily. "I feel real bad about interrupting all your fun."

"Trust me. You didn't interrupt anything. What's the message?"

"Yes, the message. Well, first of all, I wanted to tell you that I've been communicating with my cousin Dan all day long. He digs you a lot, Ms. Laruee. Holds you up to some real special level."

I smile. "Thanks, Officer Odin. That's a nice thing to say."

"No, I mean it. Dan says I can trust you. He's wanted to contact you all day himself, but he knows this isn't his jurisdiction. Plus, he's proud of me, too. We grew up more as brothers than cousins. He taught me everything he knows about the police business."

"How fortunate," I say sarcastically, though Officer Odin doesn't pick up on my tone. Officer Dan Daniel isn't exactly a shining beacon of perfect policing, but he's getting better with the more opportunities that Tucson Valley is giving him this year.

"Yeah, totally. Right? Anyway, he wanted me to tell you about a little development in the case."

"The case?"

"The case of the unidentified guy in your bathtub," Office Odin says with a confused look on his face. "You do remember, don't you?"

"Of course I remember. What's the news?"

"Well, there's been a missing person report filed in the Village of Oak Creek."

"Oak Creek?"

"Yeah, are you not from around here?"

"No, I'm a Midwestern girl transplant."

"Oh, that makes sense. Well, the Village of Oak Creek is a small town south of Sedona. And the missing person in the report matches the description of our victim: tall, skinny, businessman type, youngish. But that's not all." He's so excited he can't help but smile. And smiling about a dead body isn't exactly polite police protocol.

"The guy's name is Porter Price. He's a financial planner there. Well, at least he *was*. Had a wife."

"That's quite sad."

"Yeah, yeah, I know. But, there's more, Rosi." His eyes grow large as he moves closer, a personal space invader as he whispers his next statement. "Porter Price has a connection to Tucson Valley—a *big* one."

"Hi, Odin," says a young woman with long blonde hair down to her butt. She grabs Odin's arm, brushing her ample bosom against his chest. "I've been looking all over for you! Aren't you off the clock yet?" She looks at me and frowns.

Officer Odin blushes. "This is Bailey," he says as a way of introduction.

"Nice to meet you, Bailey," I say, irritated that my conversation with Officer Odin is being interrupted at the very moment I am about to get some potentially big news.

She ignores me and pulls at Officer Odin's arm. "Come on. They might sell out of my favorite appetizer. We need to put in our order for pork brisket nachos like yesterday. Excuse us," she says as she takes his hand and pulls him toward the bar.

Officer Odin turns around and mouths the words, *I'm sorry*. What a frustrating waste of time. What connection does Porter Price have to Tucson Valley?

## Chapter 12

After taking Barley for a short walk, she and I return to our room. I turn on the television half expecting to see a news story about the dead man found in a bathtub at a senior citizen conference in Phoenix, but I do not. Barley jumps on my bed and plops down, resting her chin in my stomach. How could a thirty or forty-year-old businessman with a wife end up *here* at this conference and lose his life in my bathtub, or at least get put into my bathtub after his life was ended? And why *my* bathtub? Do I know this guy? I lay back on the bed, propping myself up with two plump pillows as Barley begins to snooze. I pull out my phone and type in *Porter Price, Village of Oak Creek*. Images of Mr. Price in a business suit speaking at a lectern from some other conference or meeting sure look different from the Mr. Price I'd seen with a tie wrapped around his neck in my bathtub. That Mr. Price had a very bad day. The Mr. Price on the internet is smiling, one dimple on his right cheek more prominent than the other. He'd earned a couple of awards for his financial planning abilities. He'd also been a runner and gotten second place in his age group at the Tucson Valley 5k. 18:36. Not bad. There's a woman pictured next to him at a Christmas party. Her name is Danielle. I type in *Danielle Price* and discover her Facebook page. I know it's the right Danielle because there are hundreds of non-private pictures of her with Porter but with no mention of his disappearance. The most commented-on post is a shared obituary link from the Tucson Valley Funeral Home, a Mr. Roland Price. I click the link.

*Roland Price, sixty-five, of Tucson Valley, passed away at home surrounded by his son and wife, Porter (Danielle) Price. Mr. Price loved his family most of all. His hobbies included spending time with his family, golfing in his beloved retirement community where he'd made a home for himself since the passing of his darling wife, Roberta, five years ago, and building websites for friends and family. Mr. Price spent his career developing software and technology that would enhance the lives of people around the world. His life will be celebrated...*

"Hmm...what do you think, Barley? Is that the connection that Officer Odin was going to tell me about? That Porter Price's dad used to live in the Tucson Valley Retirement Community? And why does that matter?"

107

I must have fallen asleep because the sound of the hotel door opening startles me. I wipe the drool away from my mouth. Those are the best kinds of naps. Tracy throws her body face first onto her bed as if she's been pushed over. "What's the matter?" I ask, concerned for my boss and friend.

Tracy grunts in reply.

I roll Barley off my lap. She thinks she's getting a treat, so she jumps off the bed. When it doesn't come immediately, she jumps onto Tracy's bed and begins licking the back of her neck until she starts giggling. "Barley, stop. I'm upset. Barley, don't make me laugh." She rolls over, sits up, and rubs Barley's tummy as she takes a long, slow deep breath.

"What's the matter, Tracy?" I hand her a bottle of water.

She sighs. "Remember that big news I had to share tonight?"

"I remember."

"Well, nothing came of it. It was all a big waste of time."

"What was all for nothing?"

108

She throws a pillow over her head and drops back down into a prone position on the bed. "I had a really important meeting set up, and the meeting didn't go at all like I'd thought it would go after our conversation on the phone. He completely changed his mind—or my expectations were way off base."

"Can you elaborate?" I'm too tired to play a game of *what's Tracy really getting at?*

"There is a parcel of land adjoining the Tucson Valley Senior Center. It belonged to the owner of a house on the other side of the property. The only thing he had built on the parcel of land in between was a small storage shed. The board at Tucson Valley has been trying for years to figure out how to expand our community, but we are land-locked, and there aren't many options. The owner of the house didn't pay HOA dues or anything like that because his home was right outside community limits. But he joined our senior center and partook in many of our activities. You can do that for a fee. You don't have to live within the community proper to get its benefits."

"Everything for a fee," I say.

"Right, but he was a great guy. And his wife was awesome. She took tap lessons with your mom for years until her untimely death a few years ago. She was only 63." Tracy hangs her head sadly.

"And..." I prompt as I feel like Tracy is fading again.

"Oh, and he also died early—a month or so ago. His funeral was huge. I'm sure your parents would have gone if they'd been here. Cowboy Donnie's funeral services are amazing."

I recall Salem Mansfield's funeral and Cowboy Donnie's soliloquy and wonder about Tracy's assessment of Cowboy Donnie's skills.

"His son called me out of the blue two weeks ago to tell me that his dad's will had been shared with him by his lawyer. And that parcel of land, about two acres, has been donated to the retirement community."

"That's amazing! What great news!" I take a look at Tracy's face as she sits up and rubs her forehead. I realize there must be a catch. "So, what happened next?"

"We planned to meet in Phoenix and discuss the details. He had a copy of the will to share with me. The board was prepared to figure out the zoning with the city of Tucson Valley and all of the legal stuff. I was so excited to meet with him."

She pauses again, and it's driving me crazy! "Tracy, why are you so upset?" I don't mean to raise my voice, but it's been a wild twenty-hour hours.

"I just met with him in one of the empty lecture rooms. He brought the will—only it was different."

"Different, how?"

"His lawyer found an updated will giving the land to some lady named A. De LaVega."

"Who is that?"

"He said he didn't know and that he was really sorry he didn't have better news." Her shoulders fall as does her head back to the pillow. Barley rests her paws on Tracy's leg.

"Did you see the will?"

"No. Why?"

"Something doesn't sit right with me, Tracy. Something's not right." I pull out my phone which features the obituary I'd been reading before I fell asleep. "What was the name of the guy you met with?"

"Just now? The guy that dashed my dreams for the retirement community?"

"That's the one."

"Porter Price," she says. "What an odd name."

111

"That's not possible!" I say, jumping off my bed so quickly that Barley starts barking until I give her a treat. "No more, girl. Settle down."

"Why not?" Tracy sits up, the color returning to her face.

I hold my phone out to Tracy. "This is Porter Price."

"No, that man is much too young. Porter Price is older, and he's balding. That guy has a full head of hair."

I shake my head wildly. "No, no. Here is the obituary for Roland Price. I flash her the obituary notice I'd been reading. Is that the man who owned the land between the senior center and his home?"

"Yes, that's correct. Sweet Mr. Price. Roland was a wonderful man."

"Tracy, Roland was still a young man. He was only 65 when he died. You said his wife had been even younger. Did the man that you met look like he could have a 65 year-old-father?"

Tracy's eyes grow large. "Not at all. The guy I met was in his fifties or sixties! I'm so dumb! He couldn't possibly have been Roland's son."

"Don't be so hard on yourself," I say, though on the inside I'm kind of agreeing with her assessment.

"And he had the ugliest cactus neck tattoo," Tracy says as she scrunches up her nose.

"What?"

"Yes, it was quite something."

"I saw him!"

"You saw Porter Price?"

"No! I saw the man who *said* he was Porter Price, on our floor, and he ran away from me."

"Why'd he run away from you?"

"I have no idea. This doesn't make any sense," I say, dropping back to my bed.

"Then who was the guy I met with? And where is the real Porter Price?"

"I don't have an answer to your first question, but I can answer the second question." Tracy watches me expectantly. "Porter Price was the name of the man found in my bathtub last night."

"Oh, dang. That's not good. That's not good at all."

113

## Chapter 13

I won't tell Keaton any of this until I'm home tomorrow night. He will worry too much, and right now I have to get through this crazy cowboy party and meet with Officer Warren as soon as she gets back into town from her nephew's birthday party. I don't even bother with Officer Odin. Officer Daniel had texted me earlier letting me know that his cousin didn't get the brains of the family like him and that I shouldn't expect him to be much help. It took all of my inner strength to not respond with a LOL comeback. As soon as I'm dressed in blue jeans, a plaid flannel long-sleeve shirt I'd brought from Illinois when I thought I'd be here a couple of weeks in Arizona, and a moderately smashed cowboy hat that Tracy had packed for each of us, I walk down to the lobby where I am meeting with Mr. Quinta, the hotel manager. He'd only agreed to meet with me because I told him I could solve this mystery faster than the police, that I'd been a reporter in my former job, and that I had a lead that couldn't wait for Officer Warren to get back from her family birthday party. Plus, I'd promised to bring Barley with me. I'd played his emotions, but if I was correct, then I needed more proof.

All of the footage from the hotel's security system from the night of the murder has been maintained. After the inefficient security at the performing arts center in Tucson Valley delayed the resolution as to the murderer of Sherman Padowski, I'm relieved to know that video evidence exists here.

Mr. Quinta is waiting for Barley and me at the front desk. He's wearing shiny black dress shoes and a full business suit, the face of the Phoenix Emporium Hotel and Convention Center. "Hello, Barley! Who's a good puppy?" Mr. Quinta drops to the floor, reaches into his suit jacket pocket, and pulls out a dog bone for Barley to chew on. She is most grateful. Only after petting Barley and scratching her ears, does he acknowledge me. "Ms. Laruee, please follow me."

Mr. Quinta ushers us into his tiny office at the end of a corridor behind the hotel's registration desk. I'd have thought a manager at such a large hotel would have a nice office. This office is *not nice*. Aside from the pictures of what I assume to be his family hung crookedly on the wall, the décor is sparse. A fake, plastic plant collects dust in the corner of the room, and a solitary pen rests next to an otherwise empty pen container. Only one chair, Mr. Qunita's office chair, occupies the room. He tells me to take the chair while he cues up the videos I'd asked to see.

Officer Warren had told me that there was video footage of the man I now know as Porter Price entering the hotel last night while we were at the reception before the opening ceremony. He'd been seen entering his room and getting drinks in the hotel bar with a young woman around 10 p.m. He'd gone back to his room with the young woman about an hour later. Neither one of them was seen on camera again.

"I have the video lined up to the part where the victim is heading into the bar and meeting a young woman."

"Great. Thank you so much."

"I sure hope you get something more out of this than the police. This story won't hold from the media forever, and if they don't have a suspect in custody before the story breaks—oh me, oh my—I...I can't let my mind think about the crap that will hit the fan, all the conventions that will be cancelled. So, anyway," he says, clutching his heart. "Figure this out, please. I implore you."

116

"I'll do my best. Can you start the video, please?" I take off my cowboy hat and set it on the desk. I watch Porter Price walk into the bar wearing the same suit and tie he'd been wearing when he'd been found in my bathtub. It's hard to imagine that was less than twenty-four hours ago. He orders a drink at the bar—two drinks—and walks with them to a table at the back of the bar that is as far away from the security camera as possible. A woman sits at the table, anticipating his arrival, it seems. He hands her the drink. "Is there any way to zoom in on that woman?"

"Yes, I can do that to an extent. Our camera system is quite sophisticated, but they are at a table very far away from the camera."

I watch the video focus in on the woman. Her hair is long, and she wears a sleeveless fitted top. She gestures a lot with her hands as she talks, but her actual face is unclear. Mr. Quinta fast forwards the video until the point when the couple walk out of the bar about an hour later. And that's when I see it. The face, the hair, the mannerisms. Mr. Quinta sees it, too, on my face.

"Do you know her?"

I shake my head up and down. "I don't *know* her, but I've seen her. I talked to her today. Her name is Bailey."

"Oh, Lordy!" He clutches his heart again. "That woman is still in my hotel? There's a murderer still loose in my hotel. We've got to call the police. This is a large city. Officer Warren may not be available, but there are hundreds of other officers to choose from." He reaches for the phone on his desk.

"Wait. Can we finish the video first? And then you can call? Just a few minutes more, please." I smile sweetly because that can get me what I want sometimes. I'm not proud of that fact at all. I also motion for Barley with my hand so that she comes closer, brushing up against Mr. Quinta's leg with her tail which has a calming effect on him.

"Okay. The video picks up in the elevator."

I watch Porter Price, *married* Porter Price, make out with Officer Odin's new friend in the elevator. The hallway video shows him stumble toward his room, reaching into his wallet several times before he presents his hotel key and swipes the door.

"That's it. There's no more video of either of them from last night or this morning. No one comes in or out of that door again."

"Are you sure?"

"I'm calling the police and telling them that this woman is still in my hotel."

I nod my head in agreement. "I think that's a good idea. I have a stampede to attend, if you'll excuse me," I say, putting on my cowboy hat. Denial of the seriousness of this situation is my current go-to self-preservation approach. "Thank ya, Pardner Quinta."

Mr. Quinta does not smile.

"Come on, my little calf," I say to Barley as I take her outside for a quick potty break before setting her up with dinner in my room.

The Lystila Banquet Hall is decked out in western décor from the inflatable horses that line the back wall to the cacti on either side of the photo stand with props like cowboy boots and leather vests and hats (for those who didn't come with a boss prepared like Tracy who's continually surprising me with her improved organization). I tip my hat at the waiter who hands me a plate with hamburger sliders and fried pickles. He's also wearing a cowboy hat and a red bandana around his neck—with a black and white wait staff ensemble. I appreciate the effort of the staff to play along with the theme party. At least they're trying to get into the spirit. "Thank ya," I say.

119

"You're welcome," he says, eyeing me suspiciously as if I'm holding something valuable under my hat. I'm glad when he moves on to the next guest though his lingering cologne hangs in the air tickling my nose.

I step around a pair of wagon wheels set up at the end of a conference table. Mario and Leo, who have seemed to bond pretty well as the only men in our group, are chasing back bottles of beer and throwing lassos over wooden horse heads.

"Hey, Rosi, over here!" Safia, wearing a large belt buckle to hold up her long denim skirt, whistles with her fingers. The entire room goes silent for half a second.

"Hey! Glad I found you guys. There are *a lot* of people here!"

"It's a rip roarin' good time, all right," says Tracy. The tassels on her pink vest move as she talks.

Brenda, wearing a white cowboy hat, and not Tracy's provided brown cowboy hat, is sipping on a margarita. She doesn't say a word to me as she scans the crowd. Jan, however, tells me I look nice.

"So, who's going to try the mechanical bull first?" asks Leo, his eyes focused on his mayoral competition who doesn't pay him any notice.

"Not me! I've provided enough comic relief for this group of people," I laugh, finally settling into my celebrity. As expected, the number of looks I've received from strangers has already started to wane throughout the day. Some new viral sensation has taken over the world.

"I'll give it a shot!" Mario says unexpectedly. "But nobody tells Celia. She'd yell at me for chancing my bad hip."

Brooks & Dunn's "Boot Scootin' Boogie" blares from the speaker system in the walls as Mario walks into the inflatable mechanical bull pit. He expertly places his cowboy boots into the stirrups of the fake bull and swings his leg atop. The woman running the bull smiles as she begins the bull at a slow pace. But just as Mario takes off his hat and waves it in air with a *Yee-Haw*, the machine picks up speed, and he's thrown off where he bounces to a stop in the pit. The employee has to give him a hand so that he can get up. It was the kind of laugh we all needed.

"My turn!" yells Tracy. Learning from Mario's errors, she grips the leather strap around the bull's head with both hands. As she nears the evening's record time on the bull, which is posted on a sign outside the pit, the crowd surges forward.

"Go, Tracy! Go, Tracy!" Safia starts the chant.

"Woo-hoo!"

"You've got it!"

"Work it, girl!"

And lots of whistles.

"Two more seconds!" I yell.

With the bull edging to the top speed, Tracy flies off, landing on her butt with a huge smile plastered on her face.

"You did it!" I give her a big hug and a bottle of beer I snagged from the same personality-less waiter who'd given me my hamburger slider.

Safia doesn't last more than a few seconds. She slips right off but giggles so much saying *Oh, poodles* over and over that I think she still may have had more fun than Tracy. I've given up trying to understand why *poodles* is her go-to word.

After another round of drinks for our table, the music on the dance floor pulls us in for a line dancing lesson lead by none other than Dr. Rafferty Smith. I make sure to bury myself into the middle of the crowd just in case there's another Rosi mishap.

The electric slide is as basic as you can get with a line dance, but these old timers have some rhythm. Plus, the young sales marketers and presenters seem to be enjoying themselves. It's a relaxing night after a crazy twenty-hour hours. Plus, we're all here in Phoenix for one reason, to enhance the lives of seniors in the retirement stage of life. It feels good to be a part of such a positive thing.

As I'm spinning to my right, the person next to me spins to their left, sending us on a collision course of stumbling and bumbling. I fall forward, trying to catch my balance, causing the person in front of me to fall forward and so on in a domino effect of falling bodies one by one by one. As the chicken dance starts playing—does the DJ not see what's happening—I stand up. An angry woman with long blonde hair and an empty margarita glass in her hand glares at me. Her leather vest (which she wears directly over the skin of her chest) is soaked. It's Bailey.

"What the hell was that all about?" she asks, pointing her finger in my chest.

"Hey! Don't blame me. I was pushed first. Who brings full drinks onto the dance floor anyway?" I am a half second away from asking her if she murdered Porter Price

123

last night when a man comes up and puts his arm around her. It's not Officer Odin.

"Don't worry, baby. You were the cutest domino out there." He kisses her on the cheek as her eyes flutter, ratcheting down her temperature. "And this one," he says, pointing to me, "is prone to accidents. I should have warned you when I saw Rosi on the dance floor."

*Allen. Good old, dependable, horrible Allen.*

"Rosi? Her eyes grow as fast as a balloon at a party shop. "Your name is Rosi?"

I'm not about to tell her my real name is Rosisophia Doroche, my mom's invention to pay homage to her beloved Golden Girls. But before I can even say anything, she's left the dance floor, and for all I know, the party. Did she not know who I was when Officer Odin was talking to me? Did she not know that Porter Price ended up in *my bathtub?* She only knew he was deposited in a *Rosi's* room? And should I warn Allen that he may be fraternizing with a murderer? I shrug my shoulders as my friends rush to my aid and think that sometimes one should keep their mouth shut.

A consequence of my ungraceful falling on the dance floor is that, I, too, am drenched from Bailey's drink.

I excuse myself to make a quick change. I really don't want to miss the pin the spines on the cactus game. Who knew I'd get so into this silly themed party? I think it's the effects from the margaritas. I step off the elevator when the door dings, but I quickly realize I'm on the wrong floor when the giant metal cactus statue on my floor is instead an Arizona tree frog statue. The elevator next to me opens a few seconds later. I step back into my elevator and watch Adeline Vega get out of her elevator. The margaritas are controlling my impulses. I step back into the hallway. I watch Adeline turn left, and that's when I remember why the giant tree frog looks so familiar. Porter Price's room was on this floor. I wonder if they've rented it out again. How creepy, especially if he was killed there before being moved to my room.

 I walk down the hallway in the direction of Adeline. I watch her enter a room and pull out my phone. I text Mr. Quinta.

 *What room was Porter Price's?*

 His reply comes quickly. As I'm reading his answer, something hard hits my head, and I drop to the floor.

## Chapter 14

When I come to, I am sitting in a hotel room's desk chair, the kind with rolling wheels. My arms are tied to the armrests with pantyhose. My first though is, *who still wears pantyhose?*

The unenthusiastic waiter with the red bandana around his neck is sitting on the bed staring at me. His cologne hasn't dulled in its ability to overpower a room. Perhaps he's reapplied? Adeline Vega, in a long denim pencil skirt and expensive-looking cowboy boots, stands next to the window shaking her head back and forth. I clench and unclench my fists a few times, trying to make sense of this situation. The quiet gives me a minute to think. "That's it!" I yell, louder than I'd expected. "You are A. De LaVega. *You* are the woman that Roland Price's will gave his land to."

She laughs, a mocking tone, as she turns her attention away from the window and to me. "And I would have gotten away with this if it hadn't..."

"Been for me—the meddling kid?" I ask, smiling. "My morning cartoons taught me a lot."

"You are a foolish woman," she says.

"I think you can still get away with *it* or whatever the heck it is that you're doing if you untie me. I will just go back to the party as if nothing's happened. Can you do that, please?" My nerves are starting to return as my buzz diminishes.

The waiter unties the bandana around his neck revealing a large cactus tattoo.

"You're that guy! The guy that ran away from me. You really get around this hotel."

He stands up and grunts, moving closer to me to check the tightness of the pantyhose around my wrists.

"Oh! Oh! Oh! That was a mistake!" I say, putting my nose through a series of gymnastic flips to no avail. His cologne tickles the insides of my nose until I exhale a giant sneeze. "Ahhhhhcchoooo. Oops!"

"Good land, woman! What was that?"

"Sorry! I...I think I tinkled."

"You what?" Mr. Cologne yells.

"Stop! Don't get any closer, or it might happen again! I have a full bladder, and you smell! Well, you smell good, but it's too much stink, dude! I figure the longer I talk, the greater the chance that maybe Mr. Quinta will turn on the security cameras and look for me since I didn't answer his last message.

Mr. Stink looks at Adeline Vega. "It's something that happens to women," she explains.

"Especially when you've had big babies. Did you know that my son was ten po..."

"Shut up!" Adeline yells. "Stop talking!"

"Why did you do it?"

"Do what?"

"Why did you kill Porter Price?" Once I've spoken it aloud, my stomach flutters. What if Mr. Quinta doesn't turn on the cameras? What if no one finds me—until it's too late?

"Ms. Laruee, you're a nosy little mouse. And mice get snapped." She smacks her hands together. "You are in real trouble here."

I take a deep breath. "If I am in real trouble, then you might as well tell me the truth, answer my questions. What do you have to lose? Maybe airing the truth will give you some comfort, allay your guilt."

She exhales loudly. "I don't have any guilt, just that I did a poor job of planting evidence. I thought for sure your business card in Mr. Porter's shirt pocket, not to mention his BODY in your bathtub full of water and bubbles, would be a slam dunk for the police. I can't believe your reputation for dead bodies following you didn't seal the deal and land you in jail. You have more lives than a cat, Ms. Laruee."

"But why did you kill him?"

"For the same reason that Biloxi is going to kill you," she says, pointing to Mr. Stinky Cologne.

"Bill for short," he says.

"Nice to meet you, Bill."

It's the first time he smiles.

"I am the president of the Arizona chapter of the Southwest Senior Living Board, but I am also the president of the HOA board at Winding Creek Retirement Community in Saguaroville. I can't let Tucson Valley get Mr. Price's land. And with his living heir out of the way, the senior Mr. Price's land will go to me instead, the heir on the newly discovered will."

"But that's a lie."

"I know some very good forgers, and I pay my lawyer very well."

"Why do you want land in Tucson Valley when your retirement center is in Saguaroville?"

She snorts when she laughs. "I don't want that land. I want Tracy Lake and Tucson Valley to *not* have that land. Ms. Lake can't keep her mouth shut about the expansion plans she has for a state-of-the-art technological facility that would rival any in the state and further the Southwest Senior Living Board's mission for the future of seniors into realization."

"That's a good thing."

"Not when I am responsible for a rival senior community. You are so stupid."

"So, you killed a guy to protect your retirement community?"

"I'm quite benevolent, don't you think?"

"Biloxi, you'll find another pair of pantyhose in my green bag over there," she says, pointing to an open bag on the bed. "I think it will work quite well on Ms. Laruee."

"No, no, please! Wait!"

Biloxi rifles thought Adeline's bag while I try to stall with more questions. *Where is Mr. Quinta?* "How did you get Mr. Price to my room? I've…I've seen the hotel video, and he and his date were nowhere to be seen once they entered his room."

"Wait!" Adeline holds out her hand to stop Biloxi from wrapping the pantyhose around my neck. "This is a great story actually. Do you have time, Ms. Laruee?" she laughs evilly.

"All the time in the world," I whisper.

"Bailey, my niece…"

"Oh, right. That makes sense."

"Bailey has a special talent, shall me say, for the exploitation of her feminine ways. It didn't take long for her to receive an invite to Mr. Price's room."

"Which is right next to your room," I say, gesturing my head toward the door adjoining Adeline's room with the next one.

"Correct. And when my friend Biloxi delivered room service via the extra-large cart that's normally reserved for catering in the banquet halls…"

"You put Porter's body under the cart's tablecloth after he killed him," I say, nodding my head toward Biloxi who is waiting patiently to use the nylons in his hand.

"Are you telling this story or me?"

"Sorry. I was a newspaper reporter. This isn't my first rodeo." I wonder where my cowboy hat has gone. "How did you get his body into my room?"

131

"I used a key to deliver room service to the ladies next to your room," says Biloxi. "It was quite easy getting a job in the hotel."

"But they weren't there."

"Duh," he says. "You aren't very smart, are you?" He shakes his head as if he's disappointed in me. "Then I opened the adjoining door, like between these rooms," he says as she looks at the deadbolted door that connects to the room that belonged to Porter.

"I understand that the deadbolted door in Mr. Price's room would have been unlocked by Bailey, and your side would have been unlocked by Adeline, but I had my door deadlocked on my side even though you unlocked my co-workers' side of the door. How'd you get in?"

"Simple," says Biloxi.

I wait for him to continue as my worries about the passage of time are growing.

"I drilled the lock, pulled it out of the door. Then I put it back."

"Huh."

A loud pounding on the door stops Biloxi from his forward motion after Adeline had signaled for him to finish the job, meaning to finish my life.

132

"Were you expecting someone?" Biloxi asks Adeline.

"Of course I was. Don't be an idiot. It's Bailey. I told her to join us when she'd finished her night. I promised her a night of fun after all of her hard work. It really wore her out. Let's finish this mess and check out. We'll be long gone before Ms. Laruee's body is discovered."

Biloxi opens Adeline's door, but it's not Bailey on the other side of the door.

"Oh, poodles, dear! Rosi, we've been looking all over for you. Thank goodness we found your cowboy hat in the hallway. It's time to get you back to the party," says Safia, waving her hands around wildly.

"Yes, the party is not the same without you," Jan says. "The games are starting soon!"

Brenda bends over my chair, pulls a nail clipper from her purse, and begins to snip away at the nylons on my arms. She pats my arm reassuringly whispering, "It's going to by okay," as she works.

"Who the hell are these crazy women?" yells Adeline.

133

"No crazier than you, Ms. Vega," says Jan as she stands in front of her no further than a face scratch away which is exactly what she does.

"Awwww, you crazy bit…"

Safia takes her purse and slams it over the top of Adeline's head while Brenda turns toward Biloxi after she's freed one of my hands that I use to untie the other while she clips the corner of his ear with the nail trimmers.

"Stupid…Ouch!" he grabs hold of his ear while Jan uses her body as a wall to stop Adeline from fleeing.

I rummage through my purse that sits next to the television and find the pepper spray that Tracy had insisted I carry. "Ladies, get behind me!" I hold out the pepper spray, pointing it at Adeline Vega and Biloxi Cologne Man. Then I push down on the button with every bit of strength I have left. "Run!"

We run out of the doorway and straight into the people that are walking in the hallway toward Adeline's room: Mr. Qunita, Tracy, and Officer Warren, better late than never. "In there!" yells Brenda. "Those sons of a preacher man are in there!"

"Rosi! Safia! Jan! Brenda! Are you hurt?" asks Tracy.

I collapse into her arms, and soon a giant group hug of Tucson Valley Retirement Community family envelops me.

"Now, now," Safia says as she pats the top of my head.

"Nasty move with those clippers," I whisper in Brenda's ear which is still smashed against my face in Tracy's embrace.

"Thanks. I've found it's come in handy in the past."

I don't ask her any more questions.

"Yes, I'm fine. No, I was never in any real danger," I lie. "It's over, Keaton. Really, I'm coming home tomorrow morning. I promise. I won't do anything stupid. I never do. Yeah, okay, maybe that's not true. But it really is over. I have to go now. I love you, too. I'll text you when I'm in bed. I have to do a few things first. No, nothing dangerous. Yes. Yes. Goodbye for now, Keats."

"He's a keeper, Rosi," says Brenda as I click the red button on my phone.

"I know." I look into the worried faces of my co-workers. Leo and Mario have reunited with us in the hotel bar. They'd gone to look for me on the top floor while

135

Safia, Brenda, and Jan had gone from floor to floor looking for any evidence of my whereabouts after not finding me in my room. Thank goodness I'd lost my cowboy hat. Tracy had begged Mr. Quinta to view security camera footage and contacted the police as soon as they'd seen me hit over the head—with a coffee machine, no less—by the man who'd pretended to be Porter Price in Tracy's meeting when she'd been told the land would not, in fact, go to the senior center. Biloxi had a lot of jobs in this crazy plan. When Mr. Quinta had called the police to look for the woman we know as Bailey, Officer Warren had shown up—her nephew's birthday party ending early when the little guy threw up after eating too much cake. She'd been pretty hot that she hadn't been called earlier.

"I can't believe my sweet nephew Allen fell under the spell of that evil young woman," Jan says, shaking her head back and forth. "He usually has much better taste in women."

I know exactly why he chose someone like Bailey, but I don't say anything. "He's safe," I say, patting her hand.

"Yeah, we watched the whole thing go down," says Mario.

136

"That woman howled like a wolf when Officer Warren put the cuffs on her," says Leo. "It was quite a sight."

"She tried to bite Officer Warren, and that officer flipped her around so fast it was like I was watching a high action movie," says Mario.

"We can leave tonight, Rosi. No one will hold that against you," Tracy says, squeezing my hand.

"I've already missed the cowboy games. No pin the spines on the cactus for me. Do you really think I'd miss the closing ceremonies tomorrow morning?" I say because I know how much attending the entire conference and soaking in the whole experience means to my boss though I want to do nothing more than go home to Keaton.

"Well, you sure made an impression at the opening ceremonies," says Brenda dryly.

We all laugh, and it feels so good.

# Chapter 15

I hadn't gotten the sleep that I'd wanted last night. My parents had taken a long time to calm down after hearing about the murder and attempted murder at the Phoenix Emporium Hotel and Convention Center. There is no more protecting the hotel from the story even though the television in the lobby is set to Nickelodeon. Reporters had accosted Mr. Quinta and tried to get a comment on the record, but he'd done his best to rebuff them.

Most of the conference participants have gone home, intimidated by the murder that had taken place within the same building they'd slept in. But not everyone has left. A few hundred brave souls have persevered and are filling the auditorium one last time for the closing ceremonies.

Adeline Vega, president of the Arizona chapter of the Southwest Senior Living Board, is otherwise occupied in the county jail for the mastermind plot to murder Porter Price—all to stop the peaceful transfer of land from his father to the Tucson Valley Retirement Community Senior Center. Therefore, she's been removed from the itinerary.

Dr. Rafferty Smith has been asked back to give some parting remarks. Thankfully, there's been no spotting of the Screamin' Seniors.

In addition to the crazy cowboy hat that ended up saving my life, Tracy had surprised us all with matching t-shirts that said, *We won't make you. You don't have to. You're Retired. @TVRC.* The shirts, in cactus green, fit some of us better than others, but no one complained, not even Brenda. She'd just knotted hers up at the bottom on one side and added a metallic belt. The two of us haven't talked about her kindness yesterday, but I feel like we've turned a page. I still don't understand why she dislikes me so. Jealousy? A wistfulness for fading youth? And whatever Jan and Brenda had been tiffing about yesterday is gone now, too. Trauma has a way of uniting people.

"You doing okay, kid?" Mario asks as Dr. Rafferty Smith walks onstage.

"I'm great." I bang my chest. "Heart's still beating. Thanks."

"Anytime. I got your back. We all do."

"I know."

"Ladies and gentlemen, I'd like to thank you all for staying to attend the closing ceremonies. To say that this has been the most exciting conference the Southwest Senior Living Board has ever sponsored would be an understatement of epic proportions." Light laughter rises from the audience. "Yet, we have all moved forward in this weekend toward our singular goal to enhance the lives of our residents. To work in a geriatric field isn't a depressing, sad venture. No, folks. It's quite the contrary. The geriatric population in the United States and beyond is full of untapped potential, accomplishments, discoveries, hope. As a final note before we all separate back to our own communities throughout the country, I'd like to highlight one example of this forward thinking in collective work. I'd like to call Danielle Price to the stage. Please show Danielle a warm, Arizona reception."

A young woman, not much younger than me, walks slowly to the podium. She wears a tasteful black skirt and polka-dotted black and white blouse. Her strawberry blonde hair is pulled up into a high ponytail. She exudes classiness. "Thank you, ladies and gentlemen." She pauses to drink from a water bottle as she surveys the audience. "I did not know that I was going to be here until late last night. No one asked me to come. I insisted on coming. I insisted on carrying out the desire of my beloved father-in-law, Roland Price."

"Oh my word!" Tracy says quietly as she and I exchange looks.

"My father-in-law was a champion for the value of retirement communities, and his home community was literally right outside the property lines where he'd raised his family. He attended concerts, played pickleball, walked on the treadmill, joined card clubs, and met so many good people there, so many people he never would have met had he not been a part of this retirement community. Before he died, he visited with the director of Tucson Valley's Senior Center, Ms. Tracy Lake." She pauses to look at Tracy whose eyes are filling with tears. "And together they'd made a plan, a plan that, upon his death, would give Tucson Valley the land they needed to expand—to put Tucson Valley onto the map of technological innovation with the development of a state-of-the-art facility that would give seniors a chance to innovate, to engage, and to create. Ms. Lake, I'd like you come to the stage, please."

Tracy looks down at her lap where her hands are shaking.

"You look great, Tracy. Don't worry about a thing."

141

Tracy smooths her wild curls as best she can and walks slowly up the stairs to the stage where she shakes hands with Danielle Price. She waves to us. We wave back, Safia blowing kisses from her seat.

"Ms. Lake, this is the will you were to be given this weekend, the *real* will." She hands Tracy an envelope. "Our lawyers can hash out the legal details, but Tucson Valley will receive our family's land for expansion. I promise you that. And I wanted to personally represent the family in the way my father-in-law's legacy deserves. My *husband* would have given you this envelope himself but for a mishap." She clears her throat as I grab mine.

"Thank you. Thank you so much, Mrs. Price," Tracy says as she leans over the microphone. "I am honored to accept this land on behalf of my wonderful team at Tucson Valley Retirement Community. We will honor Mr. Roland Price's memory and enthusiasm for life by creating a welcoming facility that will provide our residents with the most up-to-date technological tools." She giggles. "I don't really know what those tools are yet, but I will learn, along with everyone else in TVRC!"

The crowd erupts into applause with chants of *TVRC! TVRC!* Those of us from Tucson Valley stand up and hoot and holler with such enthusiasm our voices grow raspy. Mrs. Price follows Tracy off the stage where she proceeds to shake all of our hands. When she gets to me, she whispers close, "Rosi, I've heard about your weekend. I am so sorry."

"But, your husband," I whisper back.

"My would-have-soon-been *ex-husband* was a philandering fool who got himself into this mess on his own, but my father-in-law was a lovely man. I am here for him and him alone."

"Oh," I say, sucking in my breath from surprise.

And then she walks out of the auditorium as Dr. Smith closes the conference.

## Chapter 16

The HOA board is sending a second van to pick us up this morning. No mechanical issue was discovered with the van Jan had been driving and new tires had been added, but to put her at ease, they'd sent an entirely different van. I don't really care which van I ride in. I'm tired and want to get home. "Can you watch my bags until the vans arrive while I take Barley for one last pee?"

"Sure thing, Rosi," says Mario as he maneuvers the luggage rack from Jan, Brenda, and Safia's rooms.

"Come on, Barley! Let's go." Barley wags her tail appreciatively. To my puppy, this weekend has been a glorious holiday. She'd been spoiled by the maid, Tracy, Safia, Mario, Leo, Mr. Quinta, Officer Warren, and Officer Odin. She's probably gained three pounds.

It's already in the upper 80s this morning. I wipe my forehead with the back of my hand, and Barley wiggles out of my grip as we turn the corner back to the front of the hotel. "Barley!" I yell, running after her. When I reach out to grab her leash, I realize that someone else has grabbed it. "Oh, thanks, sorry about that." I reach for the leash. "Bob? Hi! What are you doing here?" I notice the rest of the Tucson Valley Retirement Community gang congregating in the background outside the two vans that have appeared.

"Someone needed to bring the other van. I volunteered!"

"Perfect! Boys in one van. Girls in another!" says Leo.

"Brilliant idea," says Tracy enthusiastically. "But don't forget to workshop the ideas you've learned at the conference. We did real work here, team. It wasn't *all* fun and games." She laughs uneasily as she looks at me. "And please have someone take notes to share with me on Monday. I want to soak up every last bit of the things you've learned this weekend."

I think maybe Tracy would have made a great teacher.

"Got it, captain," says Mario as he puts his luggage into the back of Bob's van.

"I can't wait to hear all about it!" says Bob.

"Don't forget to have someone tell you about the disposable underwear," laughs Jan.

"Underwear?" Bob asks, wrinkling his nose.

145

"Let's get going," I say, opening the van door and putting my bags inside. "Come on, Barley."

"No, no, no! Can't that slobbery beast ride with the boys?" asks Brenda, wrinkling her nose. Barley licks Brenda's pink-painted toenails which match her tank top. She has great arms for her age. "See what I mean!" She jumps back, bumping Bob in the shoulder.

"She can ride with us," says Mario. "Come on, Barley!" Barley follows Mario into the van.

"See you all in Tucson Valley!" says Safia loudly. "Oh, poodles! Here we go!" Her face is as bright as the yellow sunflowers on her skirt.

I check the time on the dashboard as we drive away from the Phoenix Emporium Hotel and Convention Center. I'll be home by lunch. Keaton said he'd stop by in the early afternoon. That will give me time for a shower and a nap—a very long nap. I can't wait.

"Shall we begin our review of the weekend?" asks Tracy as we say goodbye to Phoenix.

"Are you serious?" asks Brenda. "Can't I close my eyes for even ten minutes before beginning your *debriefing?*"

"Nope! This ride will go quickly." She does something with her eyes that looks like an attempted wink,

146

and I wonder if she has dust in her eye. I turn my attention back to the road, hoping that since I am the driver I won't be expected to contribute as much.

"I am as serious as a bee sting in the butt!"

"Ooh, ouch!" says Safia.

"Exactly. And unless any of you want my *sting*, then let's start sharing!"

While I don't believe Tracy's sting would be as biting as *she* thinks it'd be, Jan does volunteer to share first. "Fine. I'll go. I went to a session about food and beverage service. The speaker talked about the importance of attracting food vendors to our community that serve diverse menus while at the same time being conscious of certain *needs* for the aging population."

"Like what?" I ask, playing up my role as the youngest person in the van.

Jan sighs. "You know. Like serving food with less salt or sugar and making sure that there are items that are easy to ingest."

"And chew?" asks Safia, oblivious to Jan's hesitance.

"Yes, exactly."

"That makes perfect sense," says Tracy. "As Dr. Smith talked about, the population in our communities may continue to age with advances in science and medicine, and we need to be able to service the needs of our eldest residents."

"Oh, yes! Why, I've already got partial dentures in my upper teeth."

"Safia, stop!" yells Brenda. "No one needs you to *prove it!*"

From the rearview mirror, I watch Safia drop her hands from her mouth. "Fine."

"Let's move on," says Tracy. "What did you learn, Safia?"

"Me? I already told you about how much I taught in the real estate section. Everyone learned so much from my decades of experience."

"She means, what did you *learn*—not what did you bore people with?" says Brenda dryly.

"I'll choose to ignore that comment, Brenda Riker. I learned that life is just beginning, and we can choose to make our own happiness. Hmph!"

"Don't you *hmph me*, Safia!" says Brenda.

"Ladies! Stop. I would love to hear from Tracy about the plans she has to bring Tucson Valley Retirement Community up to date with technology."

"I am so excited. With the acreage to expand upon we will have the opportunity to add a state-of-the-art technology center for our residents."

"But what does that mean exactly?" asks Jan.

"I'm not quite sure. Not going to lie. But I have a great experience pool from which to choose to help get this program off the ground. And Mr. Price and I—Roland Price—talked extensively before his passing. He painted a picture of a place with up-to-date computers for social networking, virtual reality travel opportunities, machines for monitoring health issues like high blood pressure, media centers, classes, so many things. Technology is always changing. Right, Rosi?"

"It sure is. I can't wait for this next phase of Tucson Valley."

"Oh!" says Safia.

"Oh, yes. Right," says Brenda.

"What's the matter?" I ask.

"I think we should stop for a tinkle break," says Safia. "Wouldn't want any accidents!" she laughs uncomfortably.

"Unless Rosi has a pair of disposable…"

"Brenda, stop! Someday you might appreciate that advancement in *technology*," I say, feeling the heat rise up my face. "No worries, Safia. We can stop."

"Great. Thanks, Rosi. There's a restaurant right off the next exit. It has a nice little shop inside, too. Let's go there."

"Lead the way."

I pull the van into the parking lot of the restaurant, the men's van following close behind. Barley will be happy for a potty break.

"Come along!" says Jan as she opens the van door.

The ladies walk quickly toward the restaurant. I guess they really have to use the bathroom. I walk to the men's van to retrieve Barley for her break. They are piling out for their breaks, too. "How's it going in your van?" I ask, rolling my eyes as I reflect on our experience.

"So chill, Rosi. So chill," says Mario happily.

"I even had a little snooze," says Leo as he stretches.

"Tracy will be most disappointed that you didn't do her homework."

"I'll take that chance," says Leo.

I laugh. "I'm going to take Barley for a little walk. I'll bring her back when you are done in there." Barley and I find a patch of grass under a paltry tree offering little shade in the scorching midday heat of Arizona. I realize I need to find her a bowl of water, but no one has come back outside yet. They must be doing some serious shopping in the restaurant's store. I notice an outdoor patio on the side of the restaurant with tables under large umbrellas and what looks like misting machines blowing gentle breezes onto its guests—another technological advance. I walk toward the area looking for water for Barley.

When I turn the corner, I see all my Tucson Valley team. They are seated at a long table with drink glasses filled to the brim in front of them. Barley barks and runs across the patio as I drop the leash in surprise. Keaton picks up Barley's leash and hands it to Bob. A giant bouquet of balloons bounces in the wind. Karen waves from her seat next to Bob. "What? What is happening?" I ask as a couple of stray tears fall down my cheeks because I know exactly what is happening.

Keaton holds his arms open where I go in for a hug. "Happy birthday, Rosi." He kisses me on the top of my head as I rest against his chest.

"Happy *40<sup>th</sup>* birthday!" says Tracy. "Only fifteen more years until you can buy your own condo in Tucson Valley Retirement Community!"

"And I know a great realtor!!" says Safia who is fanning herself with a napkin.

"Ah, gee, I think I'll wear out my condo a little longer, but I do know who to call." I turn back to Keats. "Thank you for the lovely balloons and nice surprise."

"I'm so glad to have you back by my side," Keaton whispers against my ear.

"I plan on staying by your side. No more wild trips in my future."

Keaton kisses me in front of everyone, and I wouldn't even mind if it went viral.

"For fruits' sake, let's eat. I'm starving. I skipped breakfast so I could save my appetite for our fancy lunch," says Brenda, shaking her head back and forth.

"You really didn't need to take me out for my birthday. Thank you all so much."

"Nonsense!" says Leo. "It's also a joint political event, so my campaign and Brenda's campaign are joining forces to treat you."

I pivot to Brenda who drops her gaze to the ground. "Is this true?"

She lets out a quick breath. "It's true—might not be legal—but it's true."

We all share a laugh, the kind only people with real connections can do, even if the connections are faulty at times.

# The Tucson Valley Retirement Community Cozy Mystery Series:

### Dying to Go (Nothing to Gush About)

Thirty-nine-year-old Rosi Laruee—named Rosisophia Doroche after her mother's beloved Golden Girls—decides that the end of her twenty-year marriage and her dad's impending knee replacement surgery are all the excuses she needs to visit Tucson Valley Retirement Community. But the drama follows Rosi when she finds the body of local tart and business owner, Salem Mansfield. The information she discovers using her newspaper reporter sleuthing skills coupled with the clues she picks up from lackluster Police Officer Dan Daniel lead to a surprise discovery when the murderer is revealed. Along the way, she meets a cast of characters in her parents' social circle who leave her questioning her parents' choices in friends while simultaneously befriending many of the residents, including a handsome landscaper and a brand-new Golden Retriever puppy she names Barley. Rosi's visit to Tucson Valley proves more than she'd bargained for, but maybe, she realizes, it's just the kind of change she needs. Laugh out loud with Rosi, and be prepared to get the happy feels along the way!

### Dying For Wine (Seeing Red)

There's a rockin' concert of 1960s impersonators coming to Tucson Valley to perform in the snowbird send-off concert at the Tucson Valley Retirement Community Performing Arts Center. And as the one in charge, Rosi Laruee is thriving in the chaos. Diva attitudes, outrageous requests, and late flights don't sideline what is meant to be the greatest concert this community has ever seen. That is, until a dead body shows up below the stage next to the front row of seats. Now, she's sleuthing again with Officer Dan Daniel. Only this time, the murder is personal, and she needs to restore the reputation of Tucson Valley as being a safe place by solving this mystery quickly. What she discovers is a much deeper web of connections than she could have imagined. Throw in a condo search, a budding relationship with Keaton, and a growing Golden Retriever to Rosi's crazy adventures, and you have a recipe for hours of laughter.

### Dying For Dirt (All Soaped Up)

It's conference time, and Rosi and her co-workers are headed to the Senior Living Retirement Community Conference in Phoenix. But don't think that it's time off! Joined by some of the most delightful and most annoying representatives of Tucson Valley Retirement Community, the trip almost ends before it begins along Interstate 10. Things don't get easier when, at the opening ceremonies, Rosi makes a most unfortunate introduction of herself. When her golden retriever puppy discovers a dead body that same night, Rosi pivots to sleuthing again as hilarity follows her every move.

### Dying To Build (Nailed It)

Coming in March 2024.

## The Secret of Blue Lake (1)

The only true certainty in life is dying, but there's a whole lot of life to live from beginning to end if you're lucky. When Chicago news reporter Meg Popkin's dad makes a surprise move to a tiny town called Blue Lake, Michigan, in the middle of nowhere and away from his family after losing his wife to cancer, she wonders if there is more to the move than *just a change of scenery*. With the help of a new, self-confident reporter at the station, Brian Welter, she tries to figure out what the secret attraction to Blue Lake is for its many new residents and along the way discovers that maybe she's been missing out on some of the joys of living herself.

*Drama, mystery, and romance abound for Meg as she learns about love, loss, and herself.*

## The Secret of Silver Beach (2)

After solving the mystery of the secret of Blue Lake, Meg returns to Chicago and to her new job as co-host on Chicago Midday. But when poor chemistry with Trenton Dealy leads to problems on the show, Meg is assigned a travel segment that will send her on location all around Lake Michigan visiting beach towns and local tourist attractions. The trip takes her away from fiancé Brian who has to continue anchoring the nightly news in Chicago. When odd threats start hurtling in Meg's direction, she finally confesses to Brian and those closest to her that she might have a stalker. Do the threats have something to do with the new information she learned about her dad's past in the little town of St. Joseph, Michigan, or is there something bigger at play that threatens more than Meg's livelihood?

# The Secret of Blue Lake:
# Chapter 1

"There's a pile up on the Dan Ryan," says my boss Jerry Stanley, his excitement for the craziest of news stories on full display. "A milk tanker collided with a truck carrying cocoa powder." He laughs, a deep hearty laugh that fills the newsroom. "I can't make this stuff up."

"Headlines writing themselves, huh?" I shake my head. It's never a dull moment at WDOU.

"Chocolate Milk Causes Road Closure on Busy Chicago Interstate," he says, smiling.

"Take a crew and talk to some people if you can—witnesses and drivers."

"Are there any fatalities?" It's the worst part of my job. Covering deaths is never easy, but since Mom died it's nearly impossible.

"No fatalities, Meg." He pats me on the shoulder. "Now get going. Take Brian with you. He needs to learn his way around Chicago," says Jerry.

I roll my eyes. The last thing I want to do is take our newest reporter Brian Welter *anywhere*. Before I can protest, I feel Brian's presence, his stale hidden-but-not-hidden cigarette stench permeating from his suit jacket. "Meggin Popkin!" He slaps the wall outside Jerry's office. "I hear I'm hanging with the number one street reporter."

I groan. No one calls me *Meggin* anymore. In a world full of Jennifers, Michelles, and Kristis, my parents bucked the trend and named their second child Megan, a different but regular-enough sounding name that they spelled M-E-G-G-I-N. I can appreciate their quest for originality, but with everyone spelling my name wrong, it was simpler to call myself Meg.

"Earth to Meggin!" Brian shouts through his cupped hands. No one should be allowed to yell at another person so closely unless in the throes of passion.

I wince at the sound of his annoying voice, ignore him, and head to my cubicle. He follows, landing in step with me. The news station abounds with energy and business, always with something going on in the Chicagoland area: the sounds of fingers on keys punching out stories or answering emails, the police scanners blaring, waiting to point a reporter to a new crime to cover, and the faint sound of elevator music playing through the overhead speakers that aim to calm the anxieties of the stories covered here.

"I'll meet you by the station van," I say. "I need to grab my phone."

"It's okay. I can wait for you. We can share an elevator. Go ahead and fix your hair, too, of course."

I know he's smiling a nauseating grin without even seeing his face. I've met this kind. I almost married this kind once before when I was young and dumb. Now I know better. But I don't get asked my opinion about new on-air talent. Even though Brian Welter comes with accolades galore for his on-air presence in Tucson, his *in-person* presence is nothing short of arrogance.

I ignore Brian as I grab my jacket along with my phone while shutting down my laptop. I have a superstition about leaving my computer on when I'm not at my desk. I don't want anyone seeing a story before it's buffed up and ready for its audience.

Brian stands to the side of the hallway as I brush past him. He rushes by to push the elevator button like a little boy fighting with his sister over who gets to push all the buttons. When Lara and I were little, we'd been assigned days. I got to do the "things" on even-numbered days while Lara got to do them on the odd-numbered days. Mom said that system cut our arguments in half. Something tells me Brian was an only child who never learned the value of compromising or perhaps the oldest who always thinks he's right. I can't help but glance in the elevator mirror before the door opens, making sure my bangs are aligned and no strands of my shoulder-length brown hair have parted on their own accord. Satisfied, I slide out the door before Brian.

Brian reaches the station van first and grabs the passenger seat door handle before I can stop him.

"No, you don't," I say, slapping my hand on the door handle, too.

"There's not room for both of us, kid." He brushes my hand away as he slips into the van.

"What an ass." I slam the backseat door.

"You'd better not mess with Meg, man," says Tom. We make eye contact through the rearview mirror. You don't make friends at a news station by ruffling the feathers of the cameraman.

*"Her?* I think I can handle *Meggin,"* he says, laughing.

"I don't need *handling*. Drive, Tom." Tom accelerates so quickly that Brian's phone slides off the dashboard and crashes into the door.

"Dammit, Tom!" he says as he reaches for his phone.

Tom, our cameraman, has been recording my news segments since I first came to WDOU five years ago. Tom and I are more than work associates. We are friends. He and his wife, Anita, were the first people in line at Mom's visitation when she died. He still brings me leftovers once a week, either extra meat he'd grilled with a side of potatoes or an extra portion of stir fry. Tom cares for me like a little sister. I know he's got my back.

I put in my AirPods before I can hear more of Brian's drivel. I watch the busy city streets pass by as we race to the scene of the chocolate milk interstate. It's easy to imagine myself living on one of those little side streets living the life of a school librarian like I'd grown up thinking I'd be. Walking the stacks, looking for the perfect alphabetical placement, sneaking in readings of newly published books. There are days when I wished I'd never gone with Dad to his job at the newspaper, when management had called for a reporter to cover the local school board meeting, and he'd looked at me and asked his boss to let me go because no one wanted the gig. And I'd gone. And I'd fallen in love with telling stories, stories of boring school board meetings to stories of convenience store break-ins to stories of interstate pileups. But some days I still wonder what it would be like living the privacy of a librarian's job without being critiqued for every outfit choice or inadvertent nose booger.

Tom grabs his camera after finally finding a place to park in a back alley between Garfield and S. Wentworth Avenue. We take the chance of getting towed, and it wouldn't be the first time. The station budgets for such expenses. *Get to the story first. Worry about the van second.*

It's a hike up the embankment to the interstate. No one should get twenty feet within distance of a Chicago interstate under normal circumstances, the cars flying miles over the speed limit, weaving in and out of traffic. But no one is moving today. I count fifteen cars that have experienced some bit of fender or bumper damage, the highway beneath our feet a cloudy brown color mixing the cocoa powder from one over-turned semi-trailer with the milk of another. I toss a glance at the side streets below the interstate and wonder again why I'm not living the life of a single librarian. It might not seem glamorous, but to me it sounds perfect right about now. The early spring temperatures in Chicago make me shiver involuntarily. I hope the chocolate milk washes away the dirty snow that lines the road. Only the first winter snow in Chicago is welcome. Every snow after lingers as a mess of dirt and trash and pollution alongside the streets for months until the temperatures warm up long enough for fresh rains to wash it away.

"Meg, you have a perspective yet?" asks Tom. He rests a camera on his shoulder and points at the scene before us, a mess of banged up-cars and trucks with people on their phones and milling around the scene talking with police and other emergency workers.

"Yeah, sorry. I'll start with that blue car. It's the closest one to the cocoa powder truck." I point to a large white truck with pictures of chocolate bars on the side. I remember that I haven't eaten lunch today. The truck is on its side, the back half blocking the right lane of traffic and the back door swung open with punctured containers of cocoa powder spilling out. The milk truck it collided with is also on its side, in the adjoining left lane with its back door open, too. Milk continues to drip down and out the truck and into the cocoa powder below.

Tom starts to follow me as I weave between cars heading to the young woman who is leaning against her car and talking on the phone. Her compact car rests against the side of the road with a bumper that looks like a large accordion after making what looks like impact with the back tire of the cocoa powder truck.

I flash my station credentials in front of her. She drops the phone to her side.

"Excuse me, miss. I'm Meg Popkin with WDOU. I'd like to ask you a few questions."

She looks at Tom who is directing his camera at her. "Okay. I can talk," she says, brushing her hands through her long brown hair, a not-so-subtle attempt to be camera ready. "I…I've been crying," she says as she looks at the camera.

I smile reassuringly. "I imagine you have. It's been a scary day."

She smiles, too, comforted by the first in-person contact she's had since the accident. "I'm Quinn," she says.

Quinn answers my questions, becoming visibly calmer as I finish learning about the accident and its effect on her. She'd been talking to her boyfriend on the phone—hands free, of course—when the collision had occurred from behind, sending her sliding into the back of the semi-truck. She's relaxed enough to laugh about the absurdity of the mess that covers the interstate. "I guess all we need now are some cookies," she says amused with her own wit.

I thank her for her time and turn to leave when Brian grabs the microphone from my hand. I hadn't even noticed he was standing behind me. "What the...?" I ask.

"Quinn, when will you be filing your lawsuit?" he asks, thrusting the microphone so close to Quinn's face it nearly knocks out a tooth.

"A what?" She wrinkles her nose and looks at me.

"Give me back my microphone," I say, trying to yank it from Brian's firm grip.

He pulls it away and back into Quinn's face. "A lawsuit," he repeats. "You stand to make a lot of money from this accident, you know?"

"I...I don't want money. I want my car fixed and to move on. This has been the scariest day of my life." She looks at me, any sense of calmness disappearing from her face.

"Shut off the camera," I say to Tom. He glances at Brian who is giving him a stink eye while shaking his head back and forth. "Shut it off, Tom," I repeat.

Tom nods his head and pulls the camera from his shoulder. He knows who the boss is here. "Thanks, Quinn. Sorry about my associate. Best wishes to you." I walk away. Tom follows.

After speaking with the driver of the milk truck and another driver who'd witnessed the collision, I'm still angry with Brian. I stomp through the chocolate milk and dirty snow back to the embankment. I sidestep my way down the hill but lose my footing on a slippery patch of snow and finish my trek down the hill on my butt. I try to stand up right away, but I slip again, this time falling forward. My pants are soaking wet. My hands are muddy, and I've lost a shoe. My day keeps getting better.

Brian arrives first at the scene of *my accident* which surprises me since he'd left my shadow after trying to mess up my interview with Quinn, his reporter's notebook hanging out of his back pocket. He doesn't hold in his laughter as he jogs down the hill behind me. "You really know how to make an exit," he says. "Here, grab my hand." He reaches his hand out to me.

I slap it away and accept Tom's help when he's rejoined us after filming more images but not shots with Brian in them. "Are you okay, Meg?" he asks, pulling me to my feet.

"I'm fine," I say too cheerily, "Nothing damaged!"

"But how's your ego?" Brian asks as he hands me my shoe.

"My *ego* is solid though not as large as yours." I stomp through the dirty snow as quickly as I can to get back to the van first and grab hold of the passenger door.

165

Tom throws me an old towel for the front seat, and I slam the door shut behind me before Brian can reply. Still, I have to give it to Brian to find another way to get the story even when the cameraman had taken my side for the day. We don't talk all the way back to the station.

"Send the tape to editing," Jerry says when I walk into the station. "We're going to run it on the 5:30 news. What took you guys so long?" he asks before seeing my muddy clothes. "What happened to you, Meg?" His eyes are as big as teacup saucers. Jerry is a great boss. Part of being a great boss it making sure things are done right and on time. And *without incident,* his favorite phrase when out on assignment.

"She bruised her bum, apparently, but not her ego, Jerry. This one's a tough cookie," Brian says gleefully.

I glare at him.

"Jerry, I have the best stories to tell," says Brian.

I purse my lips and stare at Brian. He's smiling so widely that his perfect teeth look like they'll pop out of his mouth with one swing.

"You went on camera?" Jerry asks, raising an eyebrow in surprise and ignoring my appearance for a moment.

"Well, actually I like to talk to my sources *off camera* first. Then I record my reflections on camera when I get back to the station. The camera intimidates sources from talking when they've been through something traumatic," he says, smiling as fake as the eyelashes on a Hollywood starlet.

166

I want to vomit from the acridness of his words. Plus, I really want to clean up and change clothes.

"So, I think I'll use the stationary camera I saw in the back offices to record my segment for tonight's news."

"That is ridiculous!" I can't hold back. "Jerry, I have a witness on camera who gave me an awesome interview. I talked to the driver of the milk truck. That's all we need along with Tom's shots of the scene. This isn't a major story, after all. We don't need Brian to do *anything*."

Jerry looks between Brian and me. I know he's weighing his options—keeping me happy and accommodating the new guy. "Hmm...Brian, go ahead and record your piece. Meg, take Brian's segment to editing with your segment." He sighs and curses under his breath. "You know I'm not happy about this. It's going to put us right up to news time. You are both making my job harder. If you learn to play nicely, things will be a lot easier for *all* of us." He walks away a few steps before adding. "You have 45 minutes. No exception. And clean yourself up, Meg! You look a mess!"

I death stare at Brian who has the audacity to laugh out loud. "If you play nice, you get what you want. You heard Jerry, Meg. Seems like you need to learn how to be nice. Grab a drink with me tonight, and I'll teach you how to be nice." He winks at me.

"I'd rather drink alone for the rest of my life than ever go out with you."

He snorts out loud and covers his mouth with a sickening giggle. "*That*, my dear, is not a stretch to imagine. Enjoy your solitude."

167

"You have fifteen minutes to get your part to me or the editing department won't have time to mesh it with mine!" I spit out before Brian saunters away.

I watch him walk away to record his story—my story—and dream about taking off my low black pump and throwing it at his head.

## Young Adult Historical Fiction:

## War and Me

Amazon Reviewer: *The story and characters draw you in. I felt like I was in the story and feeling the emotions of each character. I laughed. I cried. I couldn't put the book down! The story takes place during the WW2 era and intertwines love with the realities of war. A must read!*

Flying model airplanes isn't cool, not for fifteen-year-old girls in the 1940's. No one understands Julianna's love of flying model airplanes but her dad. When he leaves to fly bomber planes in Europe forcing Julianna to deal with her mother's growing depression alone, she feels abandoned until she meets Ben, the new boy in town. But when he signs up for the war, too, she has to consider whether letting her first love drift away would be far easier than waiting for the next casualties.

## Children's Chapter Books:

## Be the Vet Series

## Evie and the Volunteers Series

## Niles and Bradford Series

## Clara and Tuni Series

## Third Grade Outsider Series

## Hazel, the Clinic Cat, Series

Marcy Blesy is the author of over thirty books including the popular cozy mystery series: The Tucson Valley Retirement Community Cozy Mystery Series. Her adult romance mystery series includes The Secret of Blue Lake and The Secret of Silver Beach, both set in Michigan. Her children's books include the bestselling Be the Vet Series along with the following early chapter book series: Evie and the Volunteers, Niles and Bradford, Third Grade Outsider, and Hazel, the Clinic Cat. Her picture book, Am I Like My Daddy?, helps children who experienced the loss of a parent when they were young.

Marcy enjoys searching for treasures along the shores of Lake Michigan. She's still waiting for the day when she finds a piece of red beach glass. By day she teaches creative writing virtually to amazing students around the world.

Marcy is a believer in love and enjoys nothing more than making her readers feel a book more than simply reading it.

For updates, please click to subscribe to her newsletter.
https://preview.mailerlite.io/preview/745689/forms/108840024781358236
Follow updates on Instagram as well. @marcy_blesy


I would like to extend a heartfelt thanks to Betty for being the first person to read The Tucson Valley Retirement Community cozy mysteries and for giving me her guidance and expertise as my editor. Her personal pep talks are always welcome.

Thank you to Ed, Connor, and Luke for always championing my dreams and for believing in me. Thank you to Tom, Cheryl, and Megan for being such supports with my writing and in life.

And, finally, I'd like to think that my *Golden Girls* and *Murder She Wrote*-loving mom is smiling down on me, and perhaps, reading over my shoulder. Love you, Mom.

Made in United States
North Haven, CT
27 July 2024

55477036R00104